I0731592

OGDEN'S PROVERB

Published by Agreement with Summerfield Publishing, New Plains
Press, PO Box 1946, Auburn, AL 36831-1946

newplainspress.com
publisher@newplainspress.com

ISBN (eBook): 978-1-0879-6707-3
ISBN 13 (print): 978-1-7345719-7-4

John McCluskey 1957-

First Printing, 2022

Ogden's Proverb

JOHN MCCLUSKEY

N

NewPlainsPress.com

To mothers and fathers, to those who introduce us to
ourselves, and in memory of a friend.

"Wisdom is the principal thing; therefore get wisdom: and with all thy getting get understanding." ~ Proverbs 4:7, KJV

Yes, that's exactly when I knew, when she appeared on those basement steps leading up and out of the old garden building at Hamden Academy on what was a most notable, and quite tense (however treasurable, frankly), fatalistic Friday afternoon. Up and out and into the golden, autumn sunlight she rose, the one rich girl in prep school worth considering, who was unnecessarily nice, with ever so light sixteen-year-old blond down on her thighs, and who, thankfully, was already slated to marry the wealthiest of our classmates (and future steward, no doubt, of the economic fortunes of half the free world).

Though tagged with one of those nauseating, male-continuity-type, surname suffixes typically found in the high, holy ranks of the Hamden pecking order, that lucky bastard's full name still escapes me. But that doesn't really matter. And never really should, especially when the whole damn thing ends with a roman numeral. Any time you see "III" bringing up the rear of some fool's identity, it means nothing more than there's certainly a "IV" and then a "V" right around the proverbial Park Avenue-like corner. And, let's face it, if you're going to go that far into utter uselessness, well, a capital "V" for "Vasectomy" might be the better use of that pompously confiscated, archaic, counting system character that appeared to be quite happy on the sundial where it belonged, thank you very much, before someone who thought they knew better changed its life, giving it no say whatsoever in where it was gonna end up. I hate when you have no say in where you're gonna end up.

But, dammit, I gotta admit, young gun III was disappointingly nowhere near as disagreeable as one should be who calls upon a pretentious numbering sequence to show the world whose family really matters. (A practice, by the way, that in my estimation shoots straight to the top of the scrap heap of things that "seemed like a good idea at the time," but never really were.) In fact, he was pretty damn nice to me.

Regardless, that moment on the stairs was far more important. And, yes, she was clearly his girl, and, yes, that was perhaps the best part, but it was that teenaged blond down and genuinely peachy demeanor of hers that ended up being just the right hopelessly perfect combination I so desperately required. So long ago. Providing she was without question unavailable for public consumption, of course. She most certainly wasn't available; I was desperate for her to stay that way; she did, and, in a twinkling, I was saved. Upon those very subpar, all-weather resistant, exterior concrete steps, I was saved! Unsuccessfully, of course, but solidly and foundationally, nonetheless. And quite unavoidably, if you want to know the truth.

I felt both diminished and elated when our eyes almost met on those stairs that forever afternoon ago. Me dropping my gaze to the all too familiar territory of the tops of my worn chukka desert boots at the sound of her breathy, "Excuse me," was perfect! Who cared that all hell broke loose in the crotch of my brown corduroys at that exact, most inappropriate moment? And her speaking most sincerely through a genuine, though politely compressed smile, despite fixating squarely on the latest trophy-sized zit screaming for attention on the bridge of my sad-sack nose (and snuggling up to the remains of another blue-ribbon beauty, I might add), all too clearly indicated that she was not in the least bit interested.

Most perplexing, though, was that she was still not aware of the crushing cruelty generally required whenever the lofty paths of the forbidden intersect with that of the hopelessly lanky, the virginal, the bushy-haired, the politely pimply and anxiety-ridden. Teetering on the rookie level of advantage, no less. But, if not for Chloe, and Adam most pressingly, and a few other things that went by the wayside, I wouldn't have had to remember the late day sun finding her thighs peeking out from that sensible, plaid-skirted uniform; the musty, Friday, two o'clock air when she opened the basement door; the crack in the third stair I embarrassingly stepped over, causing the bump in my left boot, most comfortably accommodating my misbehaving little toe, to lunge dangerously close to her solidly constructed, closed-toe, left foot, saddle oxford. All occurring in that breath of a moment of deliverance.

Upon their retreat, my eyes caught a sneak peek at that supple, downy flesh, and a copy of Dante's Divine Comedy, charmingly cradled in her equally ever-so-slightly-wispy upper arms, as she surfaced from that oddly placed literature class deep in the garden catacombs of the brick fortress that was Hamden Academy, her class ending, mine just beginning.

"Abandon all hope, ye who enter here." That should have been the saying emblazoned above the entrance to pre-Harvard Hades here, not "With All Thy Getting Get Understanding." What the hell does that even mean? The only thing any of us were getting was a helluva lot of acne. And a forewarning to every new pubescent preppy that passed through those gates that some things were just not obtainable no matter how sweet their thighs, or how much of a bankroll you think Daddy has— there was always someone with more. I needed no warning, of course; her place and mine in that preordained social setup was perfect. For me.

Ah, forget Dante (but not her!). I didn't need any scholastic reminders of the "Purgatorio" I was thrust into when my fatally fulminating father rose in unexpected yet meteoric fashion to the creaky highest rungs of the proverbial East Coast corporate ladder. Without benefit of a college degree, mind you. Which

was much to my misfortune since that meant I was doomed
to have the finer things in life that he never had. Direct translation? "You're going to the best prep school around, mister.
Understand?" (With all thy getting …)

The one thing I did understand was that I always seemed to
need Orpheus-like moments at Hamden, something to over-
take my naturally despairing nature for but a breath.

Long enough to lead me up, up, and out of such a hopelessly
and embarrassingly planned life at prep school. But ascension
was not the path of my trajectory for quite some time, and
especially that day, so down I went into the bricky bowels of
higher learning, and up and out she rose.

And while I, just like Orpheus, at first, looked back at her
for that eternal, defining moment that both released and further condemned me, there she went, the real Orpheus, in an
oddly interchangeable and somewhat inaccurate role (though
certainly fitting and quite feministic), forever up and out and
back to her comfy world of honor roles and beauty to behold,
endearingly nonchalant, her quite cuddly, cradled copy of
divine, epic tragedy and comedy notwithstanding.

Of course, she never looked back, though that wouldn't have
mattered anyway because down, down, down, like a shadow,
I continued. Fittingly limp upon her departure. But, oh! so
grateful for any rise and release at all in both spirit and pants
to send me on my way, temporarily and falsely emboldened
enough to hopefully survive the week's final Literature 301
class. Still reeling from reading that troubling Rupert Brooke
poem in study hall, though. Damned meter and rhyme did
nothing to soften the connection to Adam, and it seemed to
loop in my head for days on end. Dante's "Inferno" would have
been far less torturous. No matter who was holding it.

She was holding it, of course, and the sun caught her
innocent fine hair just right, or I would have never seen it
lurking lushly beneath her nestled book of poetic hellfire,

exposing a wonderfully socially neutral and fuzzy vulnerability she seemed to unknowingly and adorably possess. Or better yet, was well aware of but didn't give a rat's ass about who saw what sprouting where! I loved that!

But who knew in that moment just before she opened the basement door and ascended through my ethereal world of despair that she was about to mean so much to me? Then and now. I shared no classes with her; I didn't see her often—rarely, in fact—a complete puzzlement, mind you, since a graduating class of only forty-four leaves little room for anonymity. (A state of being I did happen to master among this small, intimate community, and long afterwards, by the way. And quite skillfully, I might further add. Even if out of desperation.)

But had it not been necessary for me to obsess so fully and meaningfully about her, we may not have ended up so inescapably unacquainted in a one-way connection. Right when innocence was most up for grabs.

Oh, her face was fleshy and bright! Such an astounding, faintly fleecy pleasance about her! Such piliferous, post-pubescent perfection! I'm pretty sure she was the most popular girl among the titanic family names of fortune there; these were your unsinkable Astor-Guggenheim-like bunch, and easily the most desirable to those of us relegated to steerage on the good ship Hamden. But, again, ill-timed skin eruptions aside, availability was never an option equally afforded all incoming, blue-blooded, East Coast, WASPy, prep school boys sporting fresh, new, scholarly haircuts; crunching yellow maple leaves underfoot on brisk, New England, autumn mornings, secure in the fact that much less pleasingly pigmented, southeast Asian mud was never going to be underfoot in their future, even if the Vietnam lottery hadn't yet ended.

Regardless of being insulated against the annoyingly encroaching outside world, no newcomers were granted access to her charms. But I'm giving her the benefit of the doubt that her particular pleasance was always genuine and not just revealed in damp basement near misses. And certainly not the product of the secure place she held in the community of being "his girl," and the underlying knowledge that went along with it that that was for keeps.

Startlingly misplaced erection aside, which complicated my doomed fate of resignation (though not an unwelcome distraction at all), I preferred keeping my distance, after the stairwell encounter, hoping I would never run into her again during my incarceration at Hamden. It was important that I didn't.

First and foremost, I needed our near miss to remain forever unique, not diminished over time by more frequent encounters, or worse yet: the possibility of speaking, or even becoming friends. No, no, no, that could never have happened! It would have most certainly re-triggered all that day's anxiety every time I saw her. Plus, to have embraced the newly implemented, co-ed dynamics at the time, established as a test run with the Winthrop Hall Girls' School down the road, would have surely plunged me into a most unfortunate acceptance of the 'here and now.' Not only pushing my frail mother, most decidedly, over the edge with yet another societal pressure to endure, but, much more fatally, pounding with ruthless gusto the proverbial last nail in the coffin of my all too fleeting, prior, public-school life. To which my heart of hearts still clings mightily.

I chose instead to deliberately live a never-ending extension of the day I entered the Hamden locker room, after eighth grade football practice, my first year in and only year playing for "the team." Another of my rich classmates, having noticed my preference for solitary confinement over social interaction, reached out to me and attempted to welcome me into the circle through his use of a poorly timed, though amicably misplaced, and sincerely (him too?) intentioned empathy. "You'll change, Ogden Skully," he said with a disarming, though considerable, and, yes, highly unsettling, gap-toothed grin. Preferring to underscore his proclamation with my full name, lisping, whistling, and forcing it, quite unabashedly, through the queasy, dental contents of that most unappealing and, dammit, inexcusably friendly yap of his. (Thankfully for him, and most fortuitously for me, no "Skully" numerical extensions are to be found anywhere, so our mesmerizing auditory adventure remained most mercifully minimized.)

I decided in my head (to me) and with an indifferent look (to him) that I would not by any means 'change,' and I did not for my full, five years of captivity: grow, move on, let go, embrace, et cetera. So, the pattern was set that I would one day run into her in the most innocuous fashion possible, despite my groin miss-categorizing the experience as something like a hopeful, future play date, even if it did know better. My youthful, ancient heart, however, absolutely knew better, and it was already keen to the heavy stairwell air, prescient with a mysteriously satisfying sorrow and joy from the unexpected gift of safety. Bestowed through the unobtainable.

While I have to admit that in moments of weakness long after the stairwell close call, when I secretly really did want to see her from time to time, I, at the same time, wanted nothing to do with her. Why risk another Chloe? Even if she was disarmingly decent. Actually, all my classmates, male and brand-new female alike, teachers, coaches, all the upper classmen, lower classmen—everyone, regardless of platinum level lineage, right on down to kindergarten where this whole bubbled existence (for most) gets set in motion, were shockingly and confusingly, despite their general annoyances, nice, nonetheless. Including the inexplicably (considering his wealth) dentally-challenged, unapologetically breezy, straight-A-student linebacker who tried to draw me in, his after school athletic time surely better spent at the orthodontist.

And, dammit, I might as well also admit that I may have lied a wee bit when I said everybody was WASPy. Not exactly, though there were enough of them, linebacker and all, and they were quite obvious in their appearance: flush with the rosy glow of entitled and limitless futures (with unlimited cash in all cases and, in most cases, the customary full set of teeth). But while I may have looked like one of them on the outside, I certainly didn't feel like one of them on the inside—or like anyone else there. Though wanting to be desperately dissimilar, I still wondered if everybody, including myself, in that cloistered, academic environment, despite any racial, religious, ethnic, political, or developmentally stunted kinds of differences, was nonetheless pretty much the same because we all seemed to have two things in common: everyone was smart (well, mostly), and everyone came from a family with money. A lot of money.

Well, mine didn't have anywhere near the same amount as most everybody there had, I was pretty sure, so, again, I didn't think of myself as one of them, at all. I think I must have somehow slipped through the hallowed doors of educational privilege because my father had a potential for new and future earnings, though certainly not then and there, and I was sure the Hamden powers-that-be had their future eye on him.

Regardless, as I said, not everyone was WASPy, thankfully. Like the Nigerian, fraternal twins, practically admitted to Harvard on the same day they were admitted to Hamden. In the third grade! Not exactly WASPy annoying, but equally so intellectually, though again, dammit, in a nice way, if that's even possible. In any case, I couldn't stand sitting near them—they were too damn smart—let alone right next to them in class. There the three of us would be: two scintillating testaments to the benefits of a Hamden education juxtaposed with my suddenly exposed and self-aware, comparatively speaking, academic limitations. Slathered with my particular brand of social anxiety, no less, and fully on display through the use of a most uninformed seating chart (thank you very much,

Hamden). Who the hell footnotes their essay, for extra credit, with the etymology of any word over 2 syllables (their idea), one in Latin, the other in Greek? Who the hell footnotes; who the hell knows what etymology means?

And, of course, there was that classically trained baritone prodigy from the Indian sub-continent who curiously laughed unlike anyone else I ever knew: no sound from his mouth—complete silence, ironically enough, his shoulders bucking and rocking riotously every time he should have bellowed out a laugh-induced sound. Any sound would have been welcome, considering his stunning vocal range, his voice booming out so comfortably otherwise in every Hamden classical choral performance, toying mercilessly with both tenor and bass vocal ranges. Not to mention his uncanny selection of quiet hymns delivered so softly and soothingly under his breath while acing test after test, which he must have known would subliminally calm the nerves of everyone else in our small, intimate, however academically tense, classrooms, as well.

And the teachers never interfered. God, how I hate well intentioned musical prodigies that have your best interests at heart. Admirable acoustics aside, though, he was undeniably genuine. And after what he gave to Adam's family that one overwhelming day, you just couldn't discredit an agreeably gifted guy like him for possessing a teasingly silent laugh to accompany that damn, mellifluously generous heart of his.

And there were others, like the Chinese guy with but a hint of Scandinavian lineage (again, small class, everyone knew everything about everyone—except about me, as far as I could tell), fluent in English, Swedish, Danish, Mandarin *and* Cantonese, and, far more impressively, the best multi-continental point guard the Hamden basketball team ever had. And, oh, yes, to sort of even things out academically, who could forget that irritating, lower-end-of-the-bell-curve bastard from God knows where, who upon his stunning ninth grade acceptance to

Hamden, contingent upon immediate removal of the first four-teen-going-on-fifteen, visible beard the administration ever encountered, crowed most embarrassingly that he was surprisingly connected to a celebrity of sorts, hockey great Guy "Le Démon Blond" Lafleur, supposedly a direct and close relative, though our scholastically stupefied classmate was a complete disaster as a hockey player himself, seemingly singlehandedly contributing to Hamden's immediate decline in the ice sport, and being anything but Lafleuresque.

As a result, he was rightfully tagged with the hockey nickname for such useless play: "plug," personalized further by affixing the non-roman numerical (and certainly non young gun) suffix "er" quite fittingly, in his case, to produce the desired and anything but endearing "Plugger." Which everyone adopted most eagerly while conceding that, despite the good and varied populace of our frozen neighbor to the north, Canada was nonetheless clearly off the table as a viable home-land—hokey, hackneyed, hockey stereotype not-withstanding (dammit, twins, your joy of alliteration is maddeningly infec-tious).

Most assuredly, Plugger's admission to Hamden, however offensive to the logical mind, was clearly not in any way char-acteristic of ancestral lineage, athletic superiority, or academic supremacy. His admission was more like encountering a most appealing girl in a late day, autumn stairwell: something most certainly unobtainable no matter how much of a bankroll you think Daddy may have. It was quite evident that Plugger's "Daddy" had more. Much more. And out rolled the red carpet of Hamden Academy. And Plugger's clean shaven, new world. Wherever the hell he came from. No WASPy-like lie here, not even a wee bit. And, certainly, no surprise.

What was a surprise, though, was that I also ran across a few kids at Hamden from the same Italian neighborhood where I happily went to public school for a bit, before being extracted like a bad tooth and sent to bleed out all over the fucking hallways of higher learning. I didn't want to see them at Hamden because I liked keeping my early Eden Falls friends safely contained in happier days, never wanting any of them to seep into my newfound hell and thus connect those two worlds in my mind forever.

What still does and always will connect me to Hamden, however, was that kid, Adam Lastings, who, eerily, like me, sat toward the back of each class, but with his freckles and short black hair, and his constant grin, was very unlike me.

In the final analysis, I wanted no surprises, no astonishment, no cause to reconsider; I wanted them all to be the stereotypical, rich asshole—it would have been so much easier to justify my poor choice of social existence at that school. I had no idea if everyone's experience was really as harmless as it all looked because everybody seemed to fit in and like it there. Everybody, except me. Including my transplanted, public-school friends, who seemed so well acclimated that I shied away from them in my embarrassment of being further exposed. Much to their confusion. And as much as I would have liked to find someone other than myself to totally despise at that school, I couldn't. For neither ancestral, intellectual, nor traitorous reasons. They all fit in, it seemed to me, every damn one of them. Probably because they were all so rich and skied the Alps or snorkeled the Great Barrier Reef during spring break.

Or engaged in some other wealthy shenanigans, which they could all bond over during our casual Monday lunches of roast beef, mixed vegetables, and mashed potatoes, affectionately nicknamed "Mix and Mash Monday" if we had a surprise Monday math test dropped on us by Mr. Pounders, our white lab-coated, algebra teacher with a perpetual snowfall of sneezy chalk dust hovering over then settling upon his unusually small, though deceivingly wide, head. Pounders had a lunchroom nickname for every weekday, and he used them to inform us ahead of time when an upcoming pop quiz or test might be levied. He'd type his gastronomical label on the blackboard (never the same name twice in a row), killing two birds with one cruel stone by informing us of what we will be eating that day, but surely not enjoying in the least if we did have a test (no matter how soothing any accompanying hymns). The idea, of course, was to keep us studying constantly, regardless of the quantity of stomach acid produced in the process. (Again, how I hate well-intentioned musical prodigies, and now oblong-headed educators, all of whom have your best interests at heart. Gastroesophageal reflux disease notwithstanding in this particular case.)

Everybody at the table cleaned their plates gluttonously on days of false alarms, but, thanks to my anxiety, I never did, whether we had a test or not. And I, for sure, didn't ski, snorkel, golf, play squash or cricket like the other guys (well, maybe nobody actually played cricket), which made me feel even more unmasked and socially disconnected than I was willing to be comfortable with, regardless of any culinary-cute-named, pop-quiz warning signals over which a bunch of pimply, rich classmates could bond. This wasn't an issue of not being accepted, being ridiculed, left out, et cetera; it was *I* who wouldn't accept *me* being a part of *this* community. I didn't even know at that time whether I could have been a part of it successfully or not; the point was, and still is, that I wouldn't let myself in.

And why not? I was never around so many people who were so different from me before, being from other countries or other stratospheric levels of wealth. Maybe it would have been okay to know guys different from me—I thought about that. But who would have thought private school would not be exactly what you'd expect—rich and snobby.

Rich, definitely; snobby, at times, but, again, a little less WASPy, and a whole lot more welcoming than I wanted it to be. Yet even that was too much change.

I like to think that the fatal flaw here is that I am generally very loyal, though what the hell good did that do back then? Still, I could not turn my back on where I had just left–the ink was still wet. And I don't mean just the public school with the Italian kids I was talking about (well, again, perhaps a wee bit of an exaggeration: not everyone was Italian, Norman Keegler immediately comes to mind, though most memorably for a completely different, and decidedly mob-style, libidinous reason).

I had found myself once again temporarily planted quite happily and fully engaged in all activities at my new school when we first landed in Eden Falls, Connecticut, making it all the way through seventh grade before Bam! Malebolge! The eighth-grade circle of Hamden hell with all its evil ditches. Opened now beneath my every ordered, unwelcomed step (and thank you for the Italian translation, twins, in yet another of your literary appropriate languages, though you could have given my Italian friends first crack).

Yet there was something deeper than even Eden Falls public school that I would never betray: childhood in West Holland Heights, Illinois, and its overwhelming bliss. Until I turned nine years old and the business transfer for my father whisked us away to a new eastern life. But, oh! Such sweet souvenirs from the old, Dutch, onion fields of our very own Drexel Avenue!

Drexel. Brand new. Fresh, hot blacktop steaming between new, cement sidewalks deeply curbed to take away the water that fell endlessly from the black, thundering summer skies above. Strong-armed clouds, great with *aqua piovana* (enough Italian, twins!) bulged mightily before tearing a muscle and dropping the whole mess on the vast, old onion fields being built up into the homes of remembered, fleeting innocence, complete with backyard, inflatable wading pools of cold water and evening grass clippings.

All the spring and early summer rainwater brought the newly sodded grass up thick and green from the deep, rich Illinois soil. "None like it anywhere else," my father often said, especially with every clank of a shovel into the rocky, Connecticut dirt where the first order of business upon our landing in our new world was to recreate in the front yard that white birch tree he so proudly planted at our modest Midwestern home.

Though I was never quite sure of the meaning behind such a prioritized task. Or his specific sapling of choice. Was it a nod to the past to keep a clear reminder of where he came from, and just how far he came, or was he secretly aware of the symbolism involved, the birch being a figure of regeneration, hope, new dawns, et cetera? (Dammit, Hamden, why did you have to have that mini course on Celtic folklore, symbolism, and myths between semesters?) Maybe he was just a closet fan of Arbor Day, in general.

Either way, along with the new Illinois grass, the last remaining hidden onions came up, strong and smelly where the houses hadn't been built yet, and even in the middle of a few lawns of the houses already there. Thick, twisting, turning onion grass, vigorous and wily, could be found everywhere, not unlike the wayward, stray hairs poking out from the ear canals, eyebrows, and nostrils of my most mysterious Irish grandfather, coincidentally. Who clearly shaped my father's choices in life: the sorrowful and the admirable, the Midwestern and the Eastern, all of which shaped my own.

When we laid down on the lawns in the middle of our hot, youthful days, safely far out into the sea of summer back then, we'd pull up that onion grass, smell the instant aroma, and find the small, white, dirty ball at the end of the stalk. Sometimes we even unearthed a wild carrot or two. The old fragrant farmsteads where the onions were first planted couldn't have even been imagined where my house now stood, or St. Rita's elementary school around the corner, or the high school a few streets over.

We rode our bikes down those fresh, new, blacktopped streets that replaced all that aromatic acreage, settled in the mid-1800s when so many native, Netherland newcomers hit the Chicago area after a long run settling the East Coast in a kind of reverse migration from what we ourselves were about to embark upon. And, yes, I know quite a bit about this due to my father, who should have been a history teacher for his love of the subject, though that choice could not have gone well for any student in his class who dared to challenge his knowledge while he held a glass of vodka in his hand—and he would be holding a glass of vodka in his hand.

I foolishly tossed up an ill-advised objection myself one unfortunate Sunday afternoon, years later, when he most un-invitingly tried to help me with my Hamden vocabulary home-work, insisting the word narcissist had only one 's' in the middle, right after the 'ci,' while being pretty damned sure he alone was always right about these things. And pretty damned amazed at himself for how often that was, regardless of what anyone else had to say. Including me, and my attempt for accuracy by dusting off our rarely retrieved Funk & Wagnalls Standard, opening it to the page revealing the apparently questionable second 's,' and meekly presenting it to him as if it were an unfamiliar, cultural delicacy offered up on a silver platter for him to partake.

I guess I misjudged that opportunity for a possible meanin-gful moment between us. "The hell're you doing with that? I told you how to spell that damn word!" bellowed the voice of vodka, glass and ice clinking and spilling on the living room carpet while I slinked away in my usual, hang-dog posture.

What he lacked in multi-syllabic, spelling capability (with certainly no footnotes to be found anywhere, Latin or Greek) he certainly made up for with his love of history though, nailing every date, place, and battle regardless of how many 's'es were up for grabs. He even learned everything he could about West Holland Heights before we had moved there, his first home out of the city of Chicago proper, and damn proud of it, he was, puffing his ever-present, wonderfully appropriate, Dutch Masters-natural wrap-standard cigar with a sweet sense of accomplishment while surveying his kingdom, perfecto tilted upward, secured between his lips, FDR-like, in stunningly flattering, post lawn mowing, summer evening light, no less. He proudly and most sincerely imparted his newfound, neighborhood expertise upon us every chance he got, so we would live in perpetual awe of all that came before us (however long gone in a proverbial puff of smoke), and all that our surroundings might become as a result, including our short-lived place on that continuum. A pretty good existential kind of a gift he doled out, however parentally questionable the need to fill a child's head and lungs fast and loose with cognizance and carcinogens aplenty, and simultaneously at that, I might add, a certain secondhand, smoke-be-damned sensibility prevailing around teachable moments. And vodka sips, of course.

I'll bet he even knew the history behind the neighborhood nuns of St. Rita's, turning the corner most early mornings and strolling down those new sidewalks for their brisk walk, two at a time, in sweeping, wimpled strides, hands tucked and hidden into their sleeves as they passed quickly by our house then crossed the street and returned on the other side. Offering their ever-present scowl at the layman's pleasures of life directly in their path, and a glimpse of black-robed redemption should anyone be up for a spiritual lark.

A lot of new life was just starting everywhere on Drexel Avenue; not much was left of the old, but enough to smell the past and wonder if at some point all the onions would be forever gone. Or maybe a few would always stick around so that whenever the neighborhood lawns were mowed in the last light of a summer day, and we lay resplendent later in the cool, dewy, evening grass, something in the air would never let us forget. And I certainly won't, thanks to my father, despite his pathologically pollutive, prideful ponderings on the prestige of home ownership of our 6,930 square foot lot, and the rather powerfully omnipresent horticultural history that went along with it. (Though ultimately equating him with the aura of onions over cigar smoke is not going unnoticed here, and not at all fair or purposely intended, I assure you, other than to point out a meaningless irony: his cocktail garnish of choice? The ordinary over the odoriferous—the humble and harmless olive over onion, hands down.)

There was the smell of the future in West Holland Heights, too, not just the past, a harmless future, somebody else's, to be sure, but still to be savored in the here and now of your own joyfully secure existence, wafting about in the form of burnt, sawed wood. From morning till suppertime, newly framed houses buzzed with excitement. Cement poured from the circulating barrels on the backs of big, noisy trucks; wheelbarrows lumbered up planks; hammers pounded out of synch, and electric saws whined high and far off all day long. When the workmen finished their job, it was time for us to inspect, with plenty of summertime daylight left.

Great mounds of dirt were heaped up on a soon to be front lawn where surely a strand or two of its own onion grass would appear, and tightrope-like boards led you from the bumpy ground up slightly to the first floor, no front steps yet in place. Wriggle between the framed-out two-by-fours and you were in the house, the smell of sawed wood still fresh, sawdust everywhere, and rusty nails on the floor to be picked up and added to your collection. Punched out metal circles from electrical boxes always fooled us into thinking we found stray nickels—worthless, but far too shiny to discard no matter how many you found, first or second floor. And before any solid, wooden indoor staircases were installed, certainly more secure than the garden-basement-prep-school-neglected-masonry-outdoor variety type, you had to set more boards up to wobble-climb up to the second floor to get any treasures left up there.

Once there, though, the hole that would become a window was far more distracting than any flashy metal. What a view! Not so much across the open fields of the not yet fully developed neighborhood, but dizzily straight down, instead. Heads-sticking-out, two stories up, with no double hung sash windows yet installed to safely contain the inevitable, protruding, neighborhood collection of curious-young-buzz-cut-boneheaded-coconuts sticking mindlessly out, each unthinking head angled for the most precarious position possible, blissfully unaware of any potential plunge other than the headlong one into fearless independence. And not a parent in sight.

We had no concept of external dangers back then, whether inside a house or outside. We were young and magnificently so, living on the outermost rim of innocence, yes, but we didn't know that then. How could we? Post-war tract housing, subdivision growth, and other things, like high-tonnage-rail-freight-transport, for example, are, of course, your typical welcoming summer exploration opportunities for any kid; it goes without saying.

And who among us doesn't have a laughable, near miss, maiming story from not paying close enough attention when it arguably matters most. Like on train tracks. That precious, defining moment when your parents warn you to stay clear of such things (though you swear you heard, "go ahead, you'll be fine!") kicks the gates wide open. And you and your pre-pubescent posse roar through them on your Schwinn-banana-seat-butterfly-handlebar-baseball-card-spoked-stingray bikes on just another summer day with nothing better to do. Nothing better, after tiring of the dangers of new construction and backyard wading pools, than to head out into the open field near the Illinois Central train tracks, almost as far out as the "Dog'n Suds" drive-in.

In the quiet, gleaming, beaded-grass, dewy mornings we'd head for the gnarled, old, apple tree that had the nerve to pop up in the middle of all that grass and change going on around us and live forever in one spot, once as young and strong as we all saw ourselves, but now an old man bent over, trying to get out of the rain, stuck in our field and our hearts, his kind, old, branchy arms beckoning. We climbed his trunk and sat upon his timeless arms, picked his green apples, and let the day happen. It was a good place from which to start out and consider our options, but it wasn't long before we'd flee the embrace of the old man with new attention paid to the nearby train tracks and the ten thirty-five freight train out of Chicago, as dependable as fully unbridled, summer, outdoor life itself was every day. On Drexel Avenue.

Racing from tree to tracks, we'd arrive about a good ten minutes or so before the freighter was due, though none of us wore a watch. Our first inclination, every time, was to mount the rail bed, walk another tightrope, this time on the sleek and silver rails, then stroll as confident as a gunslinger down main street upon the clickety-clack ties between those endless, lustrous rails that led to new and faraway places. No train yet, we knew it, so the time was ours and we owned the rail lines. Quick! Pile up the dropped apples from the old man tree! Line 'em up on the rails like tiny, green jack-o-lanterns on a fence and wait for the great, green, applesauce smash! Lie down, ear to rail, listen for the hum, touch it, feel the vibration. Nothing yet. Soon to come, though.

Enough time for more apples, keep 'em coming, this'll be the biggest smash yet! We hurried back to the tree to get more. Then my best friend Kenny shouted out.

"It's coming!"

We all ran back to the tracks, hearts instantly abuzz, and we placed our small, sweaty palms to metal: four or five of us all in a line, quiet, breathing in an exhilarating, collective breath. And there it was, the tiniest thread of a silvery, metal buzz, the vibration growing in strength to the level of the familiar hum and feel of the transformer of my Lionel train set back home. Steadier now. Stronger. It's coming. It's coming! Once we were sure it was the freighter, we backed off, all together, at once, then turned and ran in silly, thrilling laughter to the not-so-far safety of the tree, as the Santa Fe engine slowly appeared at the farthest end of the track then grew in size, a silver-red thunderstorm building at the far end of the street.

We froze on the spot when the mighty train came roaring by, the sound alone enough to push us back beyond the tree, to our bikes, and the safety of more grassy land between us and the thundering herd. Still, we all laughed a wild joy of exuberance at the exact instant the train was at its loudest, Kenny and I side by side. Nothing we could control, though, just a purging of overwhelming excitement.

Then the sound would diminish, bringing our brains and nerves back from the point of near, total overload, slowly setting us back to the welcome, grounded feel of the security of a danger passed by. When the sound lowered enough to justify a newfound boldness, we'd return to the tracks, stand again on the rail, and watch the back end of the caboose, its shrinking image fueling the growth of our bravado.

We danced the dance of victors on the rails, whooping and hollering at the successful apple smash spread across the tracks, and we challenged a train, any train, to come by now. We'd stop it cold with our bare hands such was our fearlessness in the now harmless and gentle aftermath. And we carried on as such, from the earliest days into mid-summer, all of us taking for granted the safety of routine. Many trains had passed; many apples were smashed. Nothing to worry about. Till Jeff Spear's boldness one day took us to a new place.

At first, we raced to the tracks as usual, gathered the apples, and ran to our distant haven. The locomotive hurried by; we stood back. But as the rush of the great train blurred right in front of us, Jeff took a step forward, closer to the train, then another. And another.

"Look at me!" Jeff pounded his chest into the loud, roaring air.

"What's he doing!"

"C'mon! Nothing's gonna happen. Don't be a chicken," he challenged.

Jeff would get so close. Then he'd race along the side of the freight train, falling instantly back the moment he hit a parallel stride. It was almost comical, the tiny, running figure at the shoulder of the great train one instant, then left chasing the caboose, all in a flash. The rest of us stood our ground, unable to muster the same foolhardy courage as he, and equally unable to voice our uneasy feeling about one of us leaving the pack, going on to a bigger challenge, going his own way. Jeff raced with the trains with a growing confidence till it no longer satisfied him. Neither did the apples.

It was a cloudy morning when he hatched a new plan. The rain from the previous night left the grass marshy and soft and the rail ties slick and fast. Jeff 's younger brother, Bobby, went for the apples, but Jeff had no interest. We piled them anyway, not yet ready to surrender the familiar, and soon the pile was complete, and we took our places near the tree. Jeff moved aimlessly about, seemingly looking for new stuff. Rocks? Branches? Hey, maybe a big, old limb from the tree—it'll snap in half, watch the pieces fly!

Not good enough. Then the train appeared down the line, heading our way.

"This is getting, boring," Jeff announced.

The train seemed to be roaring up the tracks a bit faster than usual.

"Let's go get some baseball cards," someone called out into the growing noise.

"I ain't got no money," Jeff said.

"We do," Kenny yelled for both of us.

Jeff 's eyes widened. "Gimme a penny!" he said. Kenny looked at Jeff untrustingly.

"Just gimme one."

Kenny slowly pulled the change from his pocket in deference to Jeff 's determination.

"Hey!" Kenny protested anyway as Jeff grabbed a penny. "Watch this!" Jeff said.

Jeff lit out, running toward the tracks, the ten thirty-five but a hundred yards away. His instant burst of speed took his legs right out from under him on the rain-soaked grass, but he got up, ran ahead a few more yards, and knelt on the ties, focusing on a silver rail. The Santa Fe was bearing down. We heard the great horn blow down the line.

"What're you doing! Get back here!" we yelled, but the noise was too great.

Jeff set the coin down on the rail, expecting a copper, silly-putty-like prize only a train could produce.

The train sounded again.

Jeff turned around and saw the monster looming over his shoulder.

"Run! Run!" we shouted.

He broke from the tracks, got about three feet away, then slipped on the wet grass and lay flat, covering his head, too close to the vibrating rails. In an instant, the freight train roared over the spot where Jeff lost the penny.

Caught in the slipstream, we heard Jeff scream as the ferocious mix of sound and air sent great concussive waves of force rushing over him while the ground rumbled heavily beneath him.

At that wild and terrorizing moment, we turned and started to run from the scene, Bobby quite visibly scared, and we left our bikes and Jeff behind. When the train finally passed, we didn't know what to expect, but Jeff popped up in the now settling air, yelling and laughing crazily as he ran toward us in victory.

We turned to him, and his reckless, frenzied approach gave us the perfect level of permission to exhale and run back toward him to welcome home the conquering hero.

No one could face the sheer truth of the moment, the overpowering fear of what actually might've happened to him if not for three feet of slippery-safe distance, but none of us really knew what that truth was since Jeff emerged unharmed. We were convinced that since nothing had ever happened before on the tracks, nothing was ever going to happen on the tracks. Or anywhere we went. Jeff proved that.

So fully imbued with the reassurance of safety in our outdoor world, we rode our bikes fiercely and directly back to the street, cruising effortlessly once we hit blacktop again, Kenny and I with hands off the handlebars in supreme, synchronized confidence. The whole scene with Jeff was really beyond our ability to rationalize and that was the best part

We were masters of our neighborhood and at our best when away from our homes, exploring both the incomplete and the dangerous, the glorious and the shattering. We could do whatever we wanted, whenever we wanted, and it was pretty clear now that we were firmly entrenched in the good graces of the heavens above, and nothing, nothing was going to change that. And we would be back bright and early the very next morning.

Oh, so early the next morning! And the one after that, and the one after that ...

Did Jeff ever grow taller? Did Bobby ever wear his hair long? Did they stay as close as brothers are supposed to? When did my buddies start to like girls? Who moved away after me? Anyone? Anyone at all? Or did it all stay intact?

Most of all, though, did my very best friend Kenny, after chasing our Chevy as we drove away from Drexel on June 19, 1966, really shrink away out the back window while I watched?

Once we turned the corner onto 154th Street and I could no longer see him wave, did he turn back and re-enter all that Drexel Avenue was and go on without me?

I would never again see, talk to, or hear from him, but my heart to this day demands that he did, that he finished all the adventures alone that he and I were destined to witness and experience together. Neither one of us was a Jeff Spear, but both of us would always run alongside one, though now, dammit, Kenny had to do it by himself. Forever together we were supposed to stay, keeping each other safe from growing up too soon. Allies. Forever.

Ah, shit, I hate forever. Sooner or later, something always gets yanked out from underneath you, like your ever-trusting feet on some misaligned, wooden plank, or slippery, wet grass. And trusting is not something I'm gonna do again if I can help it.

I, of course, had no choice in the decision to leave Drexel Avenue for our new home, some 900 miles away in Eden Falls, not exactly a Scarsdale or Greenwich yet, but sadly on its way, so I guess I could let myself off the hook for abandoning one life and entering a new one, no matter how hard it was to look back at what I was leaving and what was leaving me. No hands and face plastered against a green Chevy's rear window, watching the Midwest streets of everlasting youth fade away behind you, except but once to endure. Over and over again. Even though that was only a moment, it still has no end. And its clingy, melancholy aftermath rode the back seat of the Chevy all the way across the Rust Belt with me and threatened to burrow a permanent home deep into the potentially positive outlook one should expect from a new beginning.

Much to my surprise, just such a beginning deceivingly presented itself once we arrived and I attended Eden Falls Elementary School, an almost Drexel-like kind of heaven, and a fresh exposure to a new, highly concentrated culture, not the same as the ones I was used to back home, of course, but still with lots of kids running around, some not speaking English at all, and it wasn't half bad. I thought I might actually find room for it in my heart along with Kenny and the onion fields, even if not yet fully embraced, like a whiskery, unknown grandfather.

But just as I settled in, I was yet again involuntarily removed, this time from a potential "East" Holland Heights kind of acceptable replacement, effectively called to turn my back on the Italian kids when the song of the private school siren reached my father's not yet gray-haired, stubbly ears, mightily betraying my fledgling willingness to trust in new places and experiences yet again, despite my earlier defiance.

All those kids yelling their asses off in the playground while I passed it by and crossed to the other side of the proverbial tracks to a proper education, to ensure my future, was too much to process for me, though apparently not for those on the playground who must've heard a similar call.

But how could I let go? Again, dammit. 'You'll change, Ogden Skully,' does nothing for the Italian kids who remained behind, and my missing place among them in the late afternoons in the schoolyard.

But leaving them, surprisingly enough, and not a moment too soon, provided quite the memorable going away present— and a most satisfactory one at that that—which I most willingly rationalized to ease the sting. It came in the form of Norman

Keegler's 11th birthday party, our last time of innocence together, courtesy of a whole new deliciously dangerous, however freight train-like, kind of thrill.

Ah, yes, Norman Keegler's party. If his gala gathering was any indication at all of the abundance of carnal joy apparently being found everywhere since the "Summer of Love," and lurking just around the pubescent corner for we partygoers as well (well ... for most of us), then perhaps that tasty, tantalizing introduction to the raging, sexual world ahead, Trojan-horsing its way into Norman's bash, was the perfect, non-academic call to change I distinctly needed to hear before I had to leave this group and head off to the scholarly advantages that beckoned, and the highly anticipated, upcoming debauchery that such a party of the future promised, no matter where you went to school. What a sendoff! Especially when you're not yet required to suit up for action!

Into the Keegler's modest home we ventured as mere boys that day, fifteen of us running amuck while the frail and ever-so-soft-spoken Mrs. Keegler tried her level best to corral us. But, to no avail. Norman's poor mother. She had no shot in hell of controlling us. Especially when Jesse Pelagatti, who snuck upstairs to the bedrooms and discovered the holy grail of Mr. and Mrs. Keegler's master bedroom, and who, at that early age, usually made an admirable attempt at English, however head-scratching (as he, himself, fluently offered up years later, post-doctoral), screamed out from the second floor in suddenly and stunningly crystal-clear English: "There's Playboys up here!"

Dead silence. Horror on Mrs. Keegler's face. Then chaos, a mob of eleven-year-old boys racing up the stairs, as newly minted men now, straight to the Keegler master bedroom, by-passing Norman's and any of his siblings' rooms as if Jesse's perfectly articulated call to arms could have only come from someplace off-limits. We burst through the master bedroom door and there it was: that glorious gallery of Playboy pinups strategically scotch-taped by Norman's father to the wall above his side of the bed, assumedly, in what he alone must have thought was a good idea. We circled that bed, which by its curious proximity to the wall-of-plenty suggested that a good night's sleep was not necessarily Norman's father's top priority. A whole new sensation was barreling down upon us now, like some brand-new, lubricious locomotive, and we had no idea at all what we were supposed to do with so much new-found visual information. But we certainly weren't going to hop on any Schwinn to escape the impact from that force—the second floor of Norman's house now so much more appealing than the immediately forgotten first floor, so hopelessly replete with the birthday paraphernalia of a suddenly and eagerly jettisoned childhood.

We gaped at that wall, as if seeing a dozen Mona Lisa's for the first time, savoring every moment we could, even while hearing Mrs. Keegler coming up the stairs, interrupting our determination to camp up there for the party's duration, and calling out in the best authoritative voice she could muster, with her desperate cry against the turning tide of innocence, "Who wants cake!"

Panic! What do we do with our newfound felicity! Didn't matter. Norman's party was a complete success

Even if we did come back downstairs dejectedly, a mortified Mrs. Keegler shooing us nervously out of her room while every pair of eyes turned for a final, fleeting, Orpheus-like look at that confusing yet enticing wall of glossy papered, undulating flesh left behind in some wildly desirable present and future deepest ring of an all too acceptable hell that we were fully wiling to inhabit, again and again, eagerly embracing our now much anticipated (and wholly, wonderfully welcome), upcoming, wanton ways. Mrs. Keegler's gentle fingers finally redirected our heads back toward the stairs, our salvation, and the birthday cake that beckoned defeatedly from atop the kitchen table, the last, lost, layered hope for an incorruptibility not already sweepingly destroyed by Mr. Keegler's complete lack of taste.

We ate Norman's now seemingly obsolete cake lustily, caught between candle glow and carnal glee, the still-raging party favors under the table so much more attention grabbing than those above it. Which Mrs. Keegler cheerlessly dispensed in the most anti-climactic fashion imaginable, once she finally gave up and sent us all into the back yard, or out into the street, or wherever the hell we wanted to go to wait for our mothers to pick us up that was anywhere but the still rabidly desired, upstairs bedroom. When we all finally left to go home, not only did we leave Norman, swelling with pride at the level of the attendees' exuberance he mistakenly assumed to be for him alone, we also left Mrs. Keegler, pondering how she would handle the inevitable influx of new friends headed Norman's way, once word got out about those most substantial, celebratory balloons incarnate plastered all over that forever joyfully corrupting bedroom wall. We all most assuredly watched her out the back window of our cars while we pulled away, Mrs. Keegler shrinking away from us, and the end of our collective innocence.

But, alas, yet another new life among a privileged, yet foreign, land awaited, requiring a complete uprooting from both my innocent, Midwest childhood and the hotly desired Norman Keegler birthday parties of the new neighborhood I so loved, and seemed to fit right into, as comfortably as a spanking new pair of age-appropriate and, thankfully, forgivingly roomy party trousers, with loudly checkered, companion shirt to match. The perfect, unassuming ensemble for both a safe, sneak peek into the end of innocence, and a newfound, hormonal-based conviction that there were some splendid, up-coming, glandular delights I had reason to believe would be heading my way at some future point. And I would be well prepared for all of them. Surely, I would, thanks to Norman's party. How could I possibly not succeed?

But away I ultimately went, in modest shirt and tie instead, lucky under the private school, autumn maples, I was repeatedly reminded, while still loyal to some misguided end, defiant to the academic call to change, and leaving forever the Italian kids (or so I thought), no hormonally-rich-delightfully-forbidden-parental-bedroom-based, neighborhood birthday parties in my rear-view mirror. But once to endure. Over and over again, dammit.

So, after a few years into this misfired attempt to better my life, was it any surprise that things would start to happen, culminating in a near miss in an old, cement stairwell on a warm, early fall afternoon with a uniform-clad girl I would have never noticed in quite the same way had it not been for Chloe? And Adam, of course. Let's not forget my father's thumb as well, pressing squarely down upon my squirmy bug-like hope for absolutely any other life than the one I had, leaving his everlasting thumbprint on my ability to process the world in a most unfinished manner. But who's to say it wouldn't have happened anyway, no matter where I went to school, parentally imposing opposable thumbs notwithstanding? My father never changed; only the schools I attended.

I never saw my father anywhere near Hamden, ironically enough. His idea of throwing me into key passages in life was to do just that: here you go! Introducing me to a new life of privileged, private, prep school was handled no differently than his father-son talk on sex. I was lying in bed doing homework behind my eternally closed bedroom door, one fateful evening, when all of a sudden there was a knock.

In one swift, nervous motion he opened the door, leaned his head in, attempted to toss an animated book on sex education onto my bed, missed, and clocked me squarely in the back of the head with it before I could even turn around to see what the hell was going on. "Read it!" he barked, and he closed the door while I was still rubbing the back of my head. And we never talked about sex again. We never talked about it at all. "Read it!" constitutes the only meaningful, bonding, informative, and intimate words ever spoken on the subject between us.

But ten seconds in my room was more time than he ever spent at Hamden. He attended no teacher conferences, no fundraisers, and none of my sporting events—as reluctant an athlete as I was (eighth grade football would have been the only shot he would have had at seeing me play). Of course, I wanted nothing to do with Hamden so there was little if any other events with me in them to attend, once again, thank you, anonymity. And, in all fairness, he was winging his way around the country in his new job, which was quite demanding, so he wasn't really all that available anyway. It was all on Mom to attend my games, and I was good, I have to admit, and he might have been surprised at what I could do out there, despite my gangly, ill-fitting, uniformed presence, including the foam rubber I stuffed into my left cleat to fill in where my little toe should normally have rested, but for some comically neurological, birth-related mystery chose to stand apart instead, slightly upright and intruding upon the space of its neighbor. Which did not, amazingly enough, impede my gait or running ability in the least. In fact, contrary to medical opinion, I believed the wayward, puny appendage was solely responsible for my swivel-hipped, incredible balance when required on the gridiron. I seemingly defied gravity while pivoting on the misshapen paw, through some form of brain-induced, silent, compensatory command, I was convinced, though my first, wet, nine-toed footprint left on the locker room floor after showering certainly put me in a state of public embarrassment that trumped any sense of earlier, future accomplishment.

Regardless, we were undefeated that year, and I did lead the team in interceptions, though I was highly reluctant to grant myself permission to enjoy the experience, or any athletic activity at that school (I was pretty good at protecting myself from any form of enjoyment), so my father might have actually been inclined to encourage me to play had he sat in those ass-pricking, splintery, wooden risers for Thursday afternoon games. Thankfully, that never happened. But he actually did make a personal appearance on campus once, though not with me present, and not for any particular event, and I liked that. I still do.

I don't know why the hell he was there, but I always liked to visualize it in completely manufactured detail to suit my memory. I still see it as a Tuesday evening in October; cocktails at the Headmaster's house; early autumn chill; a few large, yellow maple leaves already underfoot (so many maple trees around that school; that image, blond down, and my yellowed, dog-eared copy of *One Hundred Years of Solitude*, courtesy of Mr. Ungerer, which I still own despite its title most accurately and alarmingly capturing my life at Hamden, remain the only yellow things of lasting worth I took with me when I finally left that place).

And there he was, my father, in his gray business suit, my nervously exhausted mother so dutifully by his side, and the headmaster persuading him to get me to play for the school football and baseball teams next year (orthopedically designed left cleat thrown in for good measure), despite my complete and mysterious (not to me) withdrawal from playing any organized sports after eighth grade.

In no uncertain terms, he told the headmaster his son was there, first and foremost, to get a good, academic education and to prepare for college, not (a tad confusing, and surprising, I'll admit) to fill his time with other activities if he didn't want to. Admirable stance by my father, to be sure, in that apparently pre the-more-extracurricular-activities-the-better-for-college era, but his speech might have been completely unnecessary–again, had he seen me play (though that could have presented a disastrous turn of events for me)–but, realistically, he probably wouldn't have changed his laser focus on academics anyway.

Despite every new day, Monday in particular, being greeted by a first period, chalky-foggy, algebra teacher with yet another (let's just say "flavorful" in this case) predisposition; this one featuring excessively cranky, early morning bowels requiring all adolescent olfactory receptors, understandably offended by the ill winds of such perfumed higher learning, to really hold their ground for a good forty-five minutes, and ostensibly "suck it up," should any of the algebraic, competitive advantage Hamden otherwise more fragrantly offered be gained at all.

And my father, being uncannily good at math himself, surely expected I'd follow the teachings of the book of numbers just as he did, to pick up where his dream of engineering left off, or, rather, was pushed onto me without the requisite permission. So "sucking it up" was a most unfortunate and nauseatingly applicable, while critically necessary, attitude to indeed adopt in this case. And, dammit, in all fairness, how could he have possibly known of the sniff 'n sneeze classroom atmosphere at hand before recommitting me unwittingly to the challenging, floury, and effluvial, intellectual pursuit of Hamden Academy algebra?

I could've forgiven him for that, especially since his obsessiveness about my academics paired, oh so nicely, with my own for avoiding all other school activities, so we were kind of allies for the briefest, shining moment, the whole scene with the headmaster playing out, I was certain, with him never spilling a drop from his omnipresent, vodka martini. Despite the arm motions, and a somewhat animated though forceful, er ... persuasion, shall we say, of his own.

Though he really didn't flail his arms around and bellow, at least in public, I like to ensure my father did in my mind, as it properly underscores the conviction with which he drives home his point and keeps my memory of him pure and consistent. "If he didn't want to"–that's what sticks.

Though the headmaster scene is, again, left up to me to imagine as I see fit–and I do see fit to give it everything my imagination can conjure–his words were real. He told me himself, and he does not lie. I still shudder at times when I think of him standing up for me like that, especially to the headmaster of a school he so loved, and I so hated, and both of us fully aware of each other's passionate convictions. He was leaving it up to me, supporting me in whatever I decided. If I had decided to play that would have been okay, and if I didn't? That was fine, too. Obviously, but, like most things with me, I needed to repeat it over and over that way–I still do–to completely process that we apparently were on the same side ... no, that he was on my side. Without assurance of outcome! I had never been in such a position before, that I could recall. It was a generous act of unconditional support with which I was totally uncomfortable. And this ultimately, despite its initial appeal, ruined everything.

I was much more attuned to the destructive influence of second-hand vodka on my own developing mind than I was on any form of camaraderie, which perhaps was the first time I was faced with the dilemma and unwanted obligation of having to consider more than one side of my father. Even though a part of me obsessed over how he had stood up for me, I nonetheless always preferred the unfortunate comfort of a small, onion-field house back in West Holland Heights, with a black indoor railing, and a short, cement driveway outside with a '64 Chevy in it, and a father washing it on a Saturday afternoon, a glass of vodka sitting on the hot, wet, and soapy pavement, the ice inside it disappearing, and the cold, beaded glass dripping in rivers. A scene much preferable to any parental support on display at a Hamden Headmaster's house.

I had come home from playing baseball with my friends over at St. Rita's field and was delighted, though surprised, to see my father outdoors. With a hose! And spraying water! And a wet, dripping car—a lot of fun and commotion taking place on that hot driveway that I didn't typically see, nor expect to ever see at all. I didn't know what to do first: jump into the spray, help my father, or get something to drink, but I remained tentative and unknowingly suspicious of such an event free of tension. I was thirsty from the hot, dusty game, but the excitement was distracting until my father offered me a sip from his glass. This was even better than getting my own drink! I let my guard down and ran over to the cold, dripping tumbler and hoisted it high with both hands to take a big gulp from the same glass as my father—quenching more than just physical thirst—yet another surprise on such a day.

My father silently worked the hose, said nothing, and kept his attention on the car, or so I thought, until my head tilted back, the liquid poured in from an ice-clinking glass, and, in the same movement, without missing a beat, my head flew forward, and I spit out the ghastly drink with a look of utter surprise, distaste, and perhaps instant humiliation and be-trayal. My father then let out the roaring belly laugh he had so successfully contained behind the façade of dutiful work.

I was supposed to laugh along with him, and so I think I did, more in relief of the lack of stress accompanying his reaction than in any sense of fellowship, though I cannot be so sure, but it was necessary in those early days to pick up on the cue in front of you, and right away no less, and laugh (in this case) to mask any embarrassment at such betrayal.

For someone who admittedly processed emotional input at a snail's pace, I was surprisingly adept at picking up how I as-sumed I was supposed to act in order to avoid slipping and fall-ing under the roaring freight train inside our house, whether it was to laugh, or repress a totally different staircase episode yet to occur. These cues did not escape me, and I learned them, and others, instinctually, due to what I did not yet know about my father, to avoid awkwardness, discomfort, conflict, hurt, betrayal, and with the driveway vodka incident, specifically, I didn't know if I was laughing to hide my embarrassment at being tricked or to hide my embarrassment at such a juvenile joke being played by my father. As if that may very well be the best he could offer.

Either way, any little bit of betrayal to a seven-year-old boy is not a laughing matter; cruelty stings the innocent most deeply.

I would like to believe I could've shouted at him for tricking me, or maybe I could've even cried at being hurt—perhaps an overreaction, but it would have illustrated the fact that, yes, I was hurt and would not stand for it, so notice was being served. But I served no notice then, nor did my mother—how could we—though I waited endlessly for her to do so anyway and change the course of our family. But, alas, it was like waiting for that Hamden stairwell zit to end both its and my misery, hopefully without leaving a scar. But scars form. And, let's face it, they're really the only things that last.

Sadly, vodka was so prevalent in the good, old days of the good, old neighborhood—and beyond—and fueled a paternal rage that was insurmountable for the rest of the family, for so many years, that I never really thought anything of it at the time. I didn't know of the reason behind its use and had no idea what kind of home stairway incident it could cause, though clearly something was amiss in the house, it was just always there. And cues were being picked up all over the place, so the hidden message was to survive, not advertise displeasure. I guess the old, onion fields weren't quite as carefree and inno-cent as I still want them to be, when you consider that corn, and any other distillable grain, was as plentiful, apparently, as the onions themselves, just a little better preserved.

And I never forgot the taste of vodka on a seven-year-old tongue. Something so bitter and horrible tasting being so coveted by an adult, who had my life in his hands, made no sense to me. And, quite frankly, scared me a little. Had it been sweet, I would have never noticed it being anything other than that; maybe that would have been worse. But I decided at some point, though I'm still considering it, that once that wallop of a betrayal hit my unsuspecting tongue, though I had no idea at the time what introduced it into our house, and for how long it was going to hunker down, some things became unwelcomingly illuminated, some things eclipsed. And I was pretty sure I was never gonna touch the stuff myself.

Ah, vodka, the good stuff, straight from the land of Chekhov and Baryshnikov, and not an onion to be found anywhere (so much for Dutch influence). Red and white, multi-striped, candy-like, deceitful cap, the tip of the iceberg, larger cork hidden underneath it, concealing the danger, but still much more palatable to the whiskey loving US of A, and it worked! Whiskey no more! Bring on the vodka in our house, and more of it, clear as water, bottles tall as soldiers, standing guard against the evils of corn gone wrong. Then further mistreated to produce the numbing spirit required to get through life, dull the pain, trick a child on a hot driveway. Or drive to Sunday noon mass with a half tumbler of ice and the holy spirit of choice in one hand, steering wheel in the other, and a wife to play cup holder, through no choice of her own, on that rare occasion when both hands might be required on the wheel to ensure safe passage. Standing its guard, no less, clear liquid in clear glass bottles, among the darker brown beauties in the most important piece of furniture a household could proudly own throughout the postwar economic boom: the liquor cabinet. Oh, the majesty! Regal in stature, sitting atop sturdy legs, twisty spindles for décor, and the cabinet door closed and locked until further notice, keeping all at bay until Father arrived home from work.

This was the most mysterious piece of furniture to be imagined: daddy's heaven, mommy's hell, dusted begrudgingly, then left to its own devices. But in your youngest years, when that cabinet door was opened ... ah! It was like peering into the Vatican Secret Archives. Tall, saintly, secret bottles stood in humble repose; their mystery locked away for eternity. Until emptied by my-father-who-art-intoxicated, then replaced with a sense of urgency that rivaled, as an example, my mother's frantic attempt, one misbegotten, very early, family vacation to our nation's capital, to prevent a younger me from throwing up in the middle of the White House during an excessively hot and humid, crowded, late afternoon tour. Right outside Lincoln's bedroom.

She must have liked Honest Abe quite a bit because there would be no projectile vomiting on her watch, and certainly not while still within range of the sacred place of repose for The Great Emancipator himself. When nothing else seemed to stem my quickly oncoming gag responses, she bellowed out in desperation, "You will not throw up in the White House!" as both a warning to me not to put her in a position of adult responsibility for such errant public regurgitation, and a courtesy and congenial heads-up to all the other, sweat-soaked tourists in earshot to take that step back, give the kid some air, protect the tops of your shoes at all costs. Now! They did, and I didn't.

Out of either shock or respect for the most forceful display my mother ever produced, my stomach instantly settled, obeying her command much more dutifully, I might add, than did my crotch upon Mrs. Keegler's quivery request that any and all pubescent, hormonal transcendence not occur on the second floor of her house. I didn't take my eyes off my mother until we were safely escorted outside by a security guard exhibiting a similar sense of presidential respect (and an urgent professional compassion, of sorts, for the cleaning crew as well). He miraculously appeared out of nowhere at the first dry heave like some Secret Service, sanitation, SWAT team.

But oh! The scent inside that liquor cabinet back home (belying that horrid taste) before the bottles were emptied! The indoor equivalent of the onion fields and surely as reverential an experience upon that first look inside as visiting the Lincoln Bedroom during a more appetizing visit. And once the cabinet was opened, I understood the smell of liquor, that marvelous blend of spirits and wood. With such an intoxicating bouquet, how bad could it be? Maybe I was wrong. How I loved to inhale the damp, preserved air of the opened cabinet in the days before I knew what was to become of the household once the aromatic genie was let out of the bottle. How could something so harmful and sour have such a pleasing side to it? Damn it, why can't things be one way or the other, why two such opposing and conflicting sides—do you love it, or do you hate it? How are you supposed to feel? Makes it a whole lot easier to hate something when you don't have to inhale such betrayal. Or make a choice.

Of course, history has shown what my choice ultimately was at Hamden after my father's very fluid, state of the union address to the headmaster. I never set foot on a field again for a structured team sport, and he never went back on his declaration all my remaining years there, never approached the subject. How could someone rage so much and control your life in one instant yet do great things along the way as well? This fed my anxiety endlessly, not knowing which father to expect at any given moment, and whether to love or hate either one.

Maybe he was secretly glad he wouldn't have to attend games, so as not to put his stamp of approval on me risking injury or getting distracted from academics. But he may have also unwittingly fortified my position that there would be no changing going on here—I was not going to accept my new surroundings, no matter what: an unintentional green light to continue my somewhat antisocial, prep school existence. So, off I went with the free pass to misery for the next five years. For me, and for my mother.

My mother, standing at the top of the stairs in our old house in West Holland Heights, an unassuming, split-level home with a black, wrought iron railing on the stairs in the living room that led up to the bedrooms and down to a finished basement, the living room kind of like a rather large, modestly though comfortably, furnished purgatory stuck between the two: either Orpheus girl up, or loser introvert, dressed in school jacket and tie, down. Two things of interest occurred on that staircase; I was about seven years old, once again, for both of them, one being the more significant.

I liked to sit on those stairs and peer through that railing, looking straight down, just like from the window cutouts of the new houses nearby, once again secretly thrilled at the potential peril of perhaps falling through the opening, though somehow knowing I wouldn't. I'd rest my forehead in the space between two of the railing's twisty spindles, skinnier and twistier than the liquor cabinet ones, to deliberately experience the security and the dangle, that familiar conundrum of opposing sides.

One time, I pushed my head through the bars, and I felt good and daring as I slipped farther through despite the cold metal pressing against the skin behind my ears. When I realized I couldn't pull my head back, I started to panic, stuck with my head out in space, staring straight down, unable to retreat. Both Mom and Dad came to my rescue, working quietly, in tandem, to free me. No alcohol induced fuming or mishaps, just two parents together, liberating and comforting their child. I never thought much about that at the time, but it always comes back to me the further along I still go, and the more I find due cause to recognize the separation between my mother and my father, in many unspoken ways, despite their commitment to each other.

That memory sticks out as a rare glimpse into something they rallied together to do together, as silent as the pulling apart of our lives in other ways. And it seemed like everything good and bad that happened in our family happened in the heaviest weight of silence, so that when things were quiet you didn't know whether it was the good kind or the bad kind, and that was never a good setup for a kid with anxiety, or any kid for that matter.

I pulled my head back once I was freed from the spindles, like a turtle pulling his head back into the safety of its shell, never to stick out his proverbial neck again. And I never stuck mine out again, not through a railing, not in arguments with my father, certainly, or even in matters of love, I was later to discover. A dizzying thrill to look through open bars straight down, to be sure, a panic at being stuck there forever, no doubt, and a metaphor for never, ever risking one's neck, and that was the least significant episode on the stairwell. My mother standing at the top of it on yet another day far outweighs it.

Coming from the bedroom and carrying a Johnny Mathis Christmas album—her favorite, though out of season that day—my mother was crying hysterically, which I had never seen her do before. She stood at the top of those stairs, and I was the only one home with her, and I happened to be at the foot of the staircase, and I looked up and watched as she raised the record album over her head and smashed it on the same iron railing that had not so long ago caged me most mercilessly. Johnny crashed into black vinyl shards and tumbled and rained down the stairs.

She cried furiously. I watched it at seven years old. At some point, probably right afterwards, and most assuredly at the exact right time, she then came downstairs to fix me a lunchtime sandwich of peanut butter, jelly, and sorrow, and she kissed the top of my head, despite her inner turmoil, and went back upstairs after I had finished eating. I went on playing or occupying myself somewhere else in the house, and the whole incident was never spoken of, and it faded away, me never knowing what caused it, though it certainly had something to do with my father, as everything did, and this brief episode of fear and tenderness is my favorite memory of my mother.

You might think my favorite memory would be every Christmas, the only time she bounced around remarkably like a carefree child herself, despite our unsettled household, decorating, playing that LP back when it was still safely intact and Johnny's voice was indeed a tad more cheerful, embodying the childlike spirit of Christmas that she never relinquished.

Or the time during a thunderstorm when she and I were alone in the house and she retreated from the external threat breaking over our house in much the same way she did from the internal threats within our house—seeking refuge somewhere, or in something, anything, this time dragging me with her, hovering in the windowless, downstairs bathroom, terrified of impending doom. While my father always loved a good, crashing thunderstorm, my mother was frightened of them, so I was sent out of safety, between lightning flashes, to close an opened, upstairs window, and you might think that trusting me to be the only adult in that situation could be a thankful, empowerment kind of memory, but it is not.

She was much more the adult to me when crying at the top of those stairs than she was in the thundery, basement bathroom, delegating responsibility. Because she was crying alone. And I was happy to let her suffer, as an adult, in something I wasn't required to understand, or be pulled into, but trusted that, as an adult, she would bravely shield me from it, and survive it as well. And she did. Bravely. Both.

And I liked being shielded, I still do, and I preferred to hope my mother would remain a fully functioning adult after that. And if that meant the memory is one where she was suffering alone, at least I knew she was an adult because that's what we, er ... adults do.

That moment paired well, quite unfortunately, with the driveway vodka incident, further underscoring that something was amiss in the house involving my parents in some frightening, mysterious manner, which caused me to immediately root for her to make it all the way and perhaps expunge that sour, driveway taste from my tongue. She had to make it, for her sake, and mine—I needed her—but I had no idea how tall an order that was, considering my father's influence, her already somewhat mercurial constitution to begin with, and my continued involvement in episodes of her personal struggle.

My mother is born in 1928, a child in Chicago throughout the Great Depression. She is the last of eleven children and her parents are quite poor. My Polish grandfather, unlike my Irish father's father, was out of work for most of the Depression, leaving very little in terms of food and amenities for the family. She leaves for school in the morning, often without breakfast. When she gets to school, she passes out from hunger, and the neighborhood, elementary school nuns give her goat's milk to fortify her.

One Christmas she is at a school pageant, and she wins a prize! She is thrilled—she wins an orange and is the only child of her family with a gift that year. She is embarrassed by this. When she gets to eighth grade and the class is to graduate and move onto high school, she is one of many who cannot go on. And her schooling ends. She weeps in her chair in the back of the room during the ceremony. She is a good student.

She sneaks into bed to sleep between her mother and father one night when she is about the same age as I was at the bottom of that Johnny Mathis, sharded stairwell. In the middle of the darkness, she is awakened and looks up.

She sees a long dead, older brother she never knew, though recognizes from older photos, praying in the air above her mother. She is terrified and hides under the covers. When she gets enough nerve to peek back out, he is gone, and her parents sleep soundly. She tells me about this shortly before her passing so many years later.

Three of my mother's brothers and sisters die before she was born, victims of the 1918 influenza pandemic. Another one of her brothers, to whom she was very close, and who was close in age to her, was struck by a truck in the street outside their home. My mother, as a young teenager about the same age as I was at Hamden, rushes out upon hearing the noise and finds him in the street, bleeding terribly. In the ambulance on the way to the hospital, she cradles his head in her lap, bloodying her skirt. He develops epilepsy as a result of the accident, they think, yet he pulls through, but his life is now limited, including the jobs he can get. My mother remains close to him.

One afternoon, he comes home from work early and says he does not feel well. My grandmother tells him to go lie down. He goes into the front bedroom and quietly passes away.

She never talks about this, and this is my mother in non-chronological bits and pieces in the present tense of her youth, the only way I want to process her, the whole of her life surely greater than the sum of these timeless, staccato-like, selectively revealed, ancient relics I prefer, cohabitating alongside other quite unfairly demanding and isolating pieces yet to come, the logical extensions of these critical, early moments when she was young and already otherwise sadly formed. Long before the effects of an alcoholic husband got added to the mix.

But I want her young, though she is now long gone, despite the movement of time and her life, positioning both child and adult atop a wrought iron, Midwestern stairwell, or an eastern, future, front yard. Because there is joy in youth somewhere, even if tucked in the creases of cruel iniquities so seemingly carelessly and endlessly dispensed otherwise upon tiny shoulders. So, I connect with her youth, as if we are old friends looking for joy, though me and my mom's teenage experiences couldn't be more embarrassingly different. Submission. Sufferance. Respectively. And this is the museum of my choice, of my mother, her eternal selective past forever on display. In present tense.

I might as well get this out of the way right now. I have an older brother. We did a few great things together when we lived in West Holland Heights, but he was mostly interested in the neighborhood girls since he was so much older. But I didn't mind because I had my best friend Kenny and all the other kids to hang out with. When we moved to Eden Falls, and while he was still living under the same roof as us, he kind of kept more and more to himself and did what he felt he had to do to survive, not finding any refuge in anyone else in the family but behind his closed door instead, kind of like me in that regard.

He was already out of high school when we moved, luckily missing the Hamden experience altogether, but he didn't yet know what to do with himself, wasn't sure about college, and endured quite a bit of our father's wrath, head on, which I'm fairly certain ended up intensifying the focus on my demanded academic success at Hamden. But I didn't blame my brother for that. He eventually left for California, about as far away as one could reasonably get from us while remaining in the lower forty-eight, and that's all I have to say about that.

I don't think my brother was planned, nor was my mother's life, nor was my father's childhood, nor is much of anything, outside my own life, of course, that I can see, ironically enough, and I could understand how that might very well lead to a lot of difficulty for everyone later on. But the repeated instances of my young father being hit and abused as a child, which I didn't know about until much later, and long after my days at Hamden, surely had much more to do with everything I'm talking about, and it seems to me that the reach of my dark and distant Irish grandfather's hand while clenching a belt was so much longer than he could have possibly known. And that's about as far back as I can go on this, even though it leaves me wondering just when did all this really start. And there's not much more that can be said about that.

My father was born in Chicago in 1928, as well. My grandfather worked for the Illinois Central Railroad throughout the Depression, miraculously, but he worked long hours and was never home, so my father became the man of the house at the ripe old age of nine. My grandmother had to tend to my father's much younger sister, so my father was tasked with taking the streetcar alone every month to the bank downtown to pay the mortgage, the gas and electric, and any other bills, the money pinned to the inside of his coat pocket for safe keeping. He also became the handyman of the house, once again taking the streetcar, this time to the Sears Roebuck to pick up how-to pamphlets and supplies for putting in a gas line in the basement, or fixing electrical wiring, or whatever else needed attention. The pamphlets were certainly necessary, and the flawless spelling and simple, clear directions were absolutely critical.

Because even though my grandfather worked long hours, when he finally did get home after hitting all his bars on the way, often buying the house and not arriving until late, and never in good spirits, he was clearly not available for instruction, guidance, or advice, and, most definitely, not someone you'd whip out the Funk & Wagnalls for in hopes of clearing up any confusion over a possible stray "s." Those clear, concise pamphlets saved my father's hide when it came to handy work. But my father still had to look out for himself at all other times, especially when my grandfather blundered through the door late at night.

My grandfather was not a friendly drunk, to put it mildly, and my father paid the price, often beaten for no reason at the hand of his alcoholic, troubled father. My grandmother tried to stop it but could not. Whenever she heard my grandfather coming home from work, she would shoo my father out the back door, at any hour of the day or night, and he would wander the streets or back alleys through all kinds of weather, to keep out of sight and out of reach.

But he wasn't always timely with his departures, and he caught his fair share of beatings along the way, which he did not understand but endured nonetheless, fostering an anger and hatred toward my grandfather, and an unyielding love toward my grandmother. Those two became fast allies (unlike any combination of my mother, brother, and me) in order to keep the house afloat and each other safe enough from the backhand, fist, belt, suspenders, and any other paraphernalia immediately available to my grandfather, mostly by making sure enough beer was on hand at the house, ironically enough, so when he came home late any violence would be delayed until he passed out in his front room chair.

There my grandmother went, braving even the fiercest winter snowstorms, heading out with a red wagon to the nearby liquor store, younger child in tow, to get the coveted enemy of our enemy, our life-saving friend (or something like that): beer. All of this went on throughout my father's early and teen-age years, the errands to pay bills becoming more and more desperate as my grandfather drank away a good portion of his take home pay, leaving the family to fend for themselves. When my father became a teenager, and he had witnessed my grandfather striking my grandmother, he approached his father with a calm bravery, looked him in the eye, and told him if he ever touched her again, he would kill him. The violence toward her ended, and my father and grandmother were free, at least physically. But my grandfather still drank, though he pulled his apparent suffering more inward, and who the hell knows what happened to him in his life to cause all that, and the chain reaction to follow?

As a result of all his youthful responsibilities, my father became a damn good handyman over the years, doing almost anything he knew how to do with great skill. And anything he didn't know how to do with unfortunate, great confidence. This certainly benefitted our household later on, as he was indeed able to handle most anything, but my father, as talented a craftsman as he was, was not able to transfer that skill to the next generation: me. He was not a gifted teacher; not even borderline acceptable.

Any time there was Saturday work to be done around the house requiring my help there was a tenseness that rivaled the presentation of any dictionary. Helping him, or learning from him, was not an encouraging, "Now you try it," but more a conjoining of the spiritual and the scientific in a "Good Christ Almighty, don't you have a brain cell working in that head of yours!" kind of declaration that, regardless of which of those two powers you find most adequately explains the workings of the universe, ensures both were equally represented at the announcement of your particular level of generation-skipping-home-improvement ineptness.

Much to his credit, and under significantly less heated circumstances, my father frequently did, however, throw me a bone in the name of context by acknowledging this generation skip, pointing out that regardless of his father's long working hours and love for whiskey and beer he had no talent whatsoever in fixing things around the house either, so not to worry—it's not just me. Though leaving me with the realization that my grandfather and I, most queasily, have something in common, in addition to our names, doesn't quite land me in the place that I think my father was aiming for while deftly trying to navigate a soft landing on my behalf. Still, another of those damn nice things he did from time to time.

My grandfather and me. I am named after my grandfather's alias, used, as legend has it, when he ran bootleg whiskey for Al Capone at the Congress Street rail yard during the Prohibition, Ogden being a curious choice. Perhaps my grandfather was not quite nimble enough under pressure (or the influence) to produce a less conspicuous moniker, preferring instead a potentially ill-advised spotlight on his secretive, illicit activities through the use of a noticeable departure from the more common and safely lost-in-a-crowd, Irish, biblical names: John, James, Michael, Patrick, Daniel, et cetera—you can even go more ethnic without batting an eyelash: Aidan, Conan, Connor, or Cormac; what about Sean? Hell, throw in a deeper choice: Ciaran or Finn—no one's the wiser in the emerald city of Chicago—there's a helluva lot to choose from. Blend in, Grandpa! But ... Ogden? Makes you think twice at the sound of it; brings just that tad of extra attention that you clearly don't want in places with so much in common, like predominantly gangster-run railroads of 1930s Chicago, and pre-dominantly WASPy-run prep schools of 1970s Eden Falls.

Despite my grandfather's frightening and overwhelmingly dark side, my name choice is a rare, welcome memory of him. Though, admittedly, charming recollections of bouncing on old Granddad's railroad induced, arthritic knees don't exactly swell the heart with wistful longings, let alone even exist. Yet in his older days, I recall my grandfather in his Sunday suit and tie sitting alone at the kitchen table playing solitaire with a slow, trembling, bumpy hand, worn down certainly by a life not many were privileged to bear witness to in all its detail, beyond the menacing parts. And that can't be fair to my grandfather, who surely had to have survived much adversity in his life to bring him to such a dangerous place.

Maybe my best memory of my mysterious grandfather, who passed through my earlier days in the briefest fashion, was not so much the name we share, though that does connect me to him if even in the smallest way, but more his silent rise from the kitchen table upon his grandchildren's arrival in the kitchen to see what he could possibly be doing all alone in there, his slow, attention-demanding walk over to the pantry, his even slower turn toward us without saying a word (the only sound emitting from him being the ever present wheeze of the emphysema that would shortly claim him after so many years of smoking), and his long, bony finger beckoning us to follow him into the pantry, like the Ghost of Christmas Yet to Come. Showing us, in an oddly reversed and somewhat inaccurate role (not an unfamiliar dynamic to me), a far gentler, present time for us, and certainly a much better future as the first generation to be safely removed from his now tired reach.

We obeyed his call dutifully and silently, knowing this was the single, most interactive moment we would ever have with our grandfather, and he did not disappoint.

Digging into the plastic bag of hidden candy we could never on our own otherwise locate, he retrieved a Peppermint Starlight Mint for each of us, the red and white, pin-wheeled candy as forever fresh in my mind as the red and white vodka caps that forever defined our past, present and future. And so, my grandfather fades forever away, his last moments in my memory carrying the red and white flag of our family colors in the most surrendering, confectionary manner possible. And to think of my grandfather as I knew him, and my father, in their pained co-existence, whenever I see them together in a rare photo, is just something I will forever process, desperately searching for reason and comfort, but coming up empty handed all the time

—all the time. And knowing that some long, lost torment is to blame for the whole stinking mess, bleeding over from one generation to another, seemingly forever, is enough to overwhelm me whenever I think of it. So, I try not to.

But I do. Oh, I do. I must, even if I come up empty. Perhaps if I knew the sound of my grandfather's voice, something of a lasting, physical nature to linger well beyond the troubling stories, it might even now make this whole thing even more personal. I don't recall ever hearing him speak, only wheeze, so I don't know the timbre, the pitch (certainly not that of a classically trained baritone). Was it loud? Was it soft? Did it boom, was it indistinct? Was it like my father's; was it like mine in any way? There was a lot of generation skipping going on, maybe the voice, too? I don't know why it matters; I just know that it does. When all is said and done, everyone should have his or her voice remembered. It might make a difference.

While I don't have that audible memory of Gramps, I do have the triumvirate tales of the aforementioned alias, the pinwheel candy, and the family favorite gem, however fantastically fabled, which most assuredly outdoes said colorful, criminal, naming convention and elderly, bi-colored, sweetmeat disbursement: the basement, slaughterhouse fiasco.

Nobody was actually present for it other than my grandfather, so the details remain sketchy, though nauseatingly entertaining, nonetheless. We heard it many times at family gatherings, or holiday dinners, triggered by the menu staple of roast turkey, close enough to the domestic bird of choice that sadly drew the short straw one long-ago, Sunday, poultry dinner when one of my grandfather's unforeseen and rarely exhibited good intentions was entertained in the most white-knuckled fashion imaginable. Once it became apparent that an axe was to be involved.

That specific, well-intended impulse, while threatening to humanize my grandfather (despite the axe) as much as any voice would have done (and perhaps just enough to ache for him and allow your heart to remember him well while wondering whatever happened in his life to cause such alcohol abuse) nonetheless reinforced, with iron-clad resignation, that my young father was indeed doomed to handle all forms of male domesticity in his childhood home. And immediately, it should be noted, almost upon his bare-butted arrival into this world. Which my courageous grandmother most certainly must have felt she had to hasten along with a tremendous sense of urgency, given the impending stock market crash and the direction the household was alarmingly already headed, even well before she witnessed my grandfather's attempt to ease the burdens of a Sunday meal preparation by deciding, in no uncertain terms, to butcher a live chicken in the peace and quiet of the family basement.

No one seemed to know where the chicken came from—certainly they had none in the back yard—and my grandfather was not one to head to the market for any reason at all on his own, but he had one, surprisingly, and the aforementioned axe, and certainly a bottle of whiskey somewhere along the way, all of which portended a disastrous outcome. The chicken must have known something was up and that his fate was in the hands of a most unskilled executioner, under even the best of circumstances, so it managed a temporary escape from my grandfather's grasp, once indoors, and it took off.

My grandfather chased that chicken around the damp cellar till he caught it and pinned it down and, instead of holding the body down and striking a swift blow to the neck to minimize any post-traumatic, potential incident of the poor bird literally running around with its head cut off, my grandfather, in what can only be described as a temporary episode of poultry-induced-dyslexia, got the whole thing bass-ackwards, pinning the bird's head firmly to the cement instead, lowering the axe in a definitive blow, then sitting stupefied for a long moment before being called to action by a horrifically bleeding carcass, that—you guessed it—was now running around the basement headless indeed, spraying the room effusively, producing yet another chore to which my young father had to attend, this one with mop and pail aplenty.

The exhausted bird fluttered about in a final frenzy of pure nervous reaction before the inevitable sank in and the carcass fizzled out and flopped over. My crimson-coated grandfather then brought the trophy upstairs for my grandmother to continue the process of cleaning and cooking the hapless remains while he headed off to the local tavern to drown his embarrassment at the chicken getting the best of him. Despite the poorer outcome for the bird.

My grandmother, upon holding the dripping carcass over the kitchen sink, in what was perhaps the only moment she ever dared risk raising her voice to my grandfather, quite understandably bellowed out before he slinked away, "You damn fool!" Everyone still remembers my grandmother's voice.

How we loved her. And how I loved hearing that story, and the one about my name, and so many others at our Irish family get-togethers, aunts and uncles sitting around my grandmother's dining room table long after the meal was consumed, regaling the room with stories of the past, some questionably accurate, some surprising and new, all spell-binding to a handful of young cousins stopping their play in a back room when the adult laughter rose to new heights, then sneaking in unnoticed to listen to their heritage on display, wondering just who these people were that were part of your larger self, and why were some of them so much more foolhardy than others, some quiet and stern, some quite remarkable, some already long gone and never to be known, but all the beginnings of you and your cousins.

Everyone was somehow part of each other, in the late nights full of coffee, whiskey, tea with plenty of milk and sugar, laughter, tears, brogues, whiskey, borderline blasphemy upon numerous invocations of "Good Christ Almighty!" to display frustration with certain family members, and, yes, whiskey—the good, rare kind, of social connection, not of the isolated drowning of a personal angst kind. All of which lent a bit of credence to the notion that Irish storytellers may indeed be among the world's best: Joyce, Beckett, Wilde, Yeats, Binchy, O'Brien, Shaw, to name a few.

And Uncle Gogy, his proper name (to us) a deliberately shortened version of his surname, Gogarty, known to mean "banished" in some circles, which he most certainly should have been in ours, the shaving off of that middle syllable a desperate attempt to minimize the auditory annunciation required when addressing him, in the hopes that an interaction might be mercifully avoided. Abandoned syllable aside, you weren't always so lucky. His talent for wince-worthy engagement with others was fully employed at my grandfather's wake some sad years later when, shortly after our move east, the phone call came that pulled us back to Illinois for the solemn occasion.

Much old family turmoil surely passed away quietly, at last, with my grandfather, which had to have profoundly affected my father, the purveyor of such pain permanently still now in his bed of eternal rest. Even so, it certainly affected my father less so than my grandmother's passing a few years later (requiring yet another mournful return), which, upon his final moments face-to-face with her before the casket was forever closed, was the only time I saw my father openly weep. He had laid to rest his early life's ally with all the emotional strength he could muster, knowing she was now leaving him to finally fend for himself if only symbolically at that point. But her death, and perhaps being left alone with his father, was something my father had feared immeasurably during all those dangerous, younger years, and with all former threats and rescues now conclusively withdrawn upon both parent's passing, his encyclopedic early life of agony and alliance, in the making long before he was called upon to live it, had at last, and forever, passed along with them.

But Uncle Gogy saw to it that sorrow and profundity would in no way envelop my grandfather's passing. Granted, our uncle was himself getting on in years, so his judgment was certainly cloudy at best; nevertheless, he still, however ill advisedly, took it upon himself to engage the youngest mourners at the wake, my cousins and me, when he noticed we were getting a bit antsy at the sorrowful but nonetheless exciting event involving our first experience with a corpse. He had planted himself in the modest row of folding chairs reserved for family members at the head of the coffin, commandeering the seat nearest my grandfather's peaceful head, however waxy-yellowy its final skin, mesmerizing our young eyes to no end, and he beckoned us to come over in what, at first, looked like a stunningly rare and sincere effort to momentarily spell my mother, father, aunt, and uncle of their parental duty in order to allow them undisturbed time to share their grief. No one was fooled.

Due to a rare, close relationship with my grandfather, though never being one to embrace solemnity for any length of time, I'm guessing that my uncle was a bit uncomfortable at the wake, and desperately in need of some distraction himself, perhaps with a bit of the levity, however anxiety inducing, he so frequently supplied at all other family events. So, he saw an opportunity and latched onto us in what I suppose was a masked if not, however unconvincingly, admirable effort to distract the young ones in what was really an effort to deliver himself from his personal sorrow at this loss.

But his placement at the head of the casket sent up a warning flare to all, and that, coupled with his call to arms, of sorts, to gather others far younger and more curious there with him, ruled out any outside shot at a meaningful and perhaps philosophical lesson to be imparted on the next generation of the family. No wisdom whatsoever was in the wind. On the contrary, he was in rare form, and most convincingly at that, amongst both the bereaved in the sorrowful parlor containing my grandfather's remains and the men gathered in the small, adjoining room after all respects were paid, convening where there would be, of course, the requisite, small icebox packed with fresh ice for the occasion, and plenty of whiskey bottles on the shelves.

The men drank freely in there, toasting my grandfather and layering the whole affair with a raucous blend of loud camaraderie that Uncle Gogy most assuredly led, and which wafted over into the parlor with the serious mourners, our cheerfully irresponsible and alarmingly uncontrollable uncle catching the attention of my cousins and me once more. We were immediately tuned into the idea that mourning the dead was not at all as scary as it sounded, and, in fact, bested most birthday parties we had attended that year (though Norman Keegler's future party would certainly give this event a run for its money). We couldn't wait until we were older and hoped enough family members would still be around to die so we could join that room ourselves.

But before moving onto the magic of that most mysteriously desirable room, Uncle Gogy had entertained us in the parlor wholeheartedly with tall tales more suited to young minds. We lined up dutifully in front of him as he told us story after story, giggles and grins beginning to appear on our faces more and more with each telling, sending a bit of an alarm to my mother who sat across the room as reverentially as the cuting required, while keeping an eye on us nonetheless, and who was all too familiar with the proclivities of this most chancy uncle.

All seemed to go acceptably enough until Uncle Gogy let loose with the tale of how he had slipped a raw egg down some poor guy's unsuspecting throat at a most disadvantageous time, the larger story to thankfully forever remain a mystery, but that nicety alone was certainly enough to cause us to throw our collective heads back in uproarious laughter. I'm sure we cut quite an image of our four young noggins rocking back and forth in hilarity just mere inches from my grandfather's silent, sleeping head. This was perhaps a bit more than my mother had expected might occur, and she expected the worst. She shot me fierce glances to control my laughter while clearly caught in the dilemma of whether that would be sufficient, or should she bring even more attention to the matter by coming over to break up the party. She opted for the death stare instead.

But you remembered those events, despite their questionable occurrences, and you listened. Not only to understand more about your Irish self, but your Polish self as well, over similar gatherings across town, my mother's side of the family so pleasingly full of the same kind of laughter, tears, and revelations at the expense of long gone relatives, over the dining delights of pierogies, paczki or kolaczki (sometimes both), but never the dreaded czernina: duck's blood soup that you never tried, or even saw, but heard ghastly stories of its precise and careful preparation to avoid unfortunate clotting at any point during its presentation and consumption. The namesake ingredient alone conjured up kindred images of your crosstown Irish grandfather's poultry pursuits, and things like Irish wakes and mysterious, plasmatic Polish soups were the great things that belonged to you because of who you were, and all who came before you to make you who you were. And those things, most unfortunately, were the very first to get tossed aside with the onion grass and the neighborhood spirit of growing up during the move from our heritage rich homeland of Illinois to our new more sanitized home, with no connection anymore to anything that came before us. Except, of course, for the whiskey, or vodka, in our case, which never left us no matter where we had lived, and I often wondered why my father's choice of alcoholic escape departed from the whiskey-loving, larger family's beverage of choice, but I guess, based on his childhood, he wanted to get away and be distinctly different in every way possible from his Irish heritage and upbringing. Even in matters of self-distraction, or self-destruction.

Regardless, it seem like some big mistake if you have to lose a part of who you already are just to gain a new part that you might not even want. Whenever I think of this, I still think of the Italian kids at my first school in Eden Falls, and it struck me as the same type of thing to get yanked out of that, and I'm not even Italian, and maybe the twins and the baritone got yanked out of somewhere, too.

Come to think of it, we all probably did, maybe even Plugger, though that would certainly be no loss whatsoever to the small, local community of his North American origin. Wherever the hell that was. Getting yanked out of stuff is something I have come to loathe. And uprooting to Eden Falls gave me something else to loathe: helping my father home-improve our brand new, heritage-free house.

Not too long after we moved in, my father decided to turn our damp basement into a finished room, working on weekends, with me reluctantly in tow. It was incredible to me that he found any time at all to work on the house, considering the job he eventually rose into. My grandfather's stormy influence on him, accompanying us east after leaving its Midwestern debris field behind, unwittingly caused my father to go as high up and as far away as he could to reinforce his self-worth through an admirable, though sadly ineffective, attempt to replace alcoholic pain mitigation with a non-alcoholic option: successful career advancement.

Such mitigation, however, required a transfer to the southwestern-most tip of Connecticut, close to Manhattan where he worked ultimately as an executive, rising remarkably to that level without benefit of a college degree at all but managing and working with, for, and alongside Ivy leaguers, and others of various college pedigree.

This was an astounding deliverance of sorts, considering my father's past, of course, and he thrived in New York, eventually meeting all challenges, and he ultimately exceeded them quite convincingly, after a bit of a low-confidence, shaky start, it should be noted. Which my mother managed to erase, boosting his confidence, encouraging him, while managing a young family in a new, unknown, and highly uncomfortable environment, and while also associating with women of substantial collegiate pedigree as well, which she, like my father, did not share.

But she rose to the occasion, despite the toll it took on her, and thus we headed off into the unknown world of elite privilege and surrounding wealth, and a pressure to which we all were unaccustomed. To which more vodka was inevitably still required to stem the patriarchal pains constantly beneath the surface of my father's very being, and which, most sadly, a change in scenery and responsibilities alone could not finally cleanse away.

Hard as he tried to sincerely grow into a newer self, he was nonetheless increasingly tested with new, unfamiliar pressures in a corporate culture of martini lunches and dinners, and while he most fully, and admiringly so, achieved the successful corporate advancement part of the newer self equation, the very last thing our family needed was a work-culture-inspired, free-weekday-pass to more alcohol. Or a weekend spent helping 'Good Ol' Dad' around the house.

To start the basement refurbishing, we (he) had saw horses set up in the basement; we (he) measured the 2x4's and paneling to be put up (the most contemporary brand that 1969 right on up through 1973 could offer), and he started to cut the paneling to size, bending over the saw horses and firing up the electric saw while I stood dutifully to the side to hopefully watch and learn, though there was minimal watching, and certainly no learning going on, whatsoever.

As he engaged saw with wood, the high-pitched whine, much less desirable now than that from Illinois new construction, drowned out every sound around us, except the critically and, most importantly, father (not son) uttered, "Fuck!" shouted quite audibly while trying to be simultaneously contained when he realized the measurement was off and had stopped the saw at the most revealing, auditory moment. Still bending over his work, and once the saw quieted and the room was now uncomfortably silent, he raised an eye and looked over at me upon successful completion of everyman's common expression of frustration when something goes wrong.

That was the longest and most awkward eye contact I ever made with my father, his glance up at me certainly intending to certify that I had not heard his go-to profanity of choice for compromised critical calibrations, proclaimed without missing a beat, mind you, and leading one to believe that as handy as my father was, the rare "Fuck!" of miscalculation was nonetheless a tool as easily accessible as any hammer, screwdriver, or wrench so otherwise easily employed.

But I'm certain he knew I heard it, and his eye lift had put me in the distressing position of either acknowledging that most forgivable error, by nodding back and risking a camaraderie of sorts (which would have never happened), or looking around as if I hadn't heard it and did not see him look up, thereby saving both of us the embarrassment of an eye contact neither of us wanted to make at that moment, but which was now unfortunately out there and fully punctuated by the ensuing silence.

Surprisingly, considering the presence of vodka in the house, I don't believe I had ever heard my father use any word stronger than "hell" or "damn" up to that point, and certainly not the crown jewel, "Fuck!" at all, regardless of how many blown measurements belonged to his past without an audience nearby. And hearing your father say that word in no uncertain terms and with clear intent, and so close to you before you are of age to laugh it off together, if that was ever even possible with him, was not at all the bonding moment you both might look back on years later and relive over a beer.

I stood by nervously, not knowing what to do with my eyes or hands, but, somewhat to my surprise, I did happen to notice that when my father finally pulled his glance away, and went back to the task at hand, his instinctive look at me was not an admonishment to not say a word, nor a friendly eye-lock that secretly said, "Let's keep this between us." He looked embarrassed at being caught in front of his child, revealing his lack of self-control. I did not like seeing my father embarrassed by his eye level being below mine, inadvertently giving me for a fleeting, incorrect moment a position of potential higher moral authority, which I did not want at all. Especially at the expense of my father's momentary loss of self-esteem, which, years later, I recognized as being the first time I was in such a position. I would never, ever, let myself be in that position again, I swore, if I could help it. I would not be his equal, could not be above him in anything at all. It was much too uncomfortable and insecure a place to be. I preferred instead the safety and familiarity of an alcohol-accompanied cohabitation with my father, fully accepting my emotional residence of choice.

At that time, I still knew nothing yet of his upbringing, or my grandfather's proclivity toward inebriation and violence at the expense of my father—that would come much later. But I did know by then that my father was volatile too, and he possessed a most frightening temper as well, so there was no reaction that could have been produced in that basement, or anywhere else, for that matter, other than the complete stillness required whenever anything unplanned occurred around him. And that must certainly be why I would remember such a small, otherwise forgettable and laugh-awayable moment, so oddly favorably—it offered clarity as to whom I might be.

I'm pretty sure seeing my father in that moment failed to generate any early buoyancy of spirit, however subconscious at that age, or the necessary nudge of confidence that, one day, you will, as everyone must, leave your father's side and emerge as your own independent person. But I never wanted to leave. I was anxious, he was not; I was timid he was not; I could not take care of myself—I was already convinced—he was more capable; I was weak, and he was strong. I was all of these things under the impact of my father (and grandfather, another generation away) and their desperate attempts to liquefy their pain away, but that pain defined them both. And it defined me, too.

Perhaps there were early, similar signs about my father that my mother missed regarding his rage, but it would have been difficult to notice them given the circumstance under which they met. He had planned upon graduating from high school that he would study engineering in college, yet fate did not comply. In addition to dealing him a poor hand at childhood, my father was further rewarded with yet another obstacle to overcome: a severe case of TB in his teenage years, causing him to be sent to the san for a while in order to heal. This almost killed him. He had lost about 40% left lung capacity during that ordeal, which years later did nothing to stop his heavy chain smoking—the evil twin to his drinking—but certainly ended his dream of studying engineering, the doctors insisting the stress would kill him. And me and my dad's teenage experiences couldn't be more embarrassingly different. Unsalvageable. Unbreakable. Respectively.

Interestingly enough, my mother went into the san at about the same time, though that was her second trip.

When she was about nine or ten, she too had picked up a case of TB, hers from a neighborhood girl she often played with and whose father had the disease and sat in their front room by the window every day to keep an eye on his young daughter playing outside. You could see him coughing quite often in the window, as apparently my grandmother did when passing by their house regularly on her way to the market.

Soon his daughter started coughing, too. My grandmother was very keen to the dangers of TB, which was running rampant at the time, and she warned my mother to stay away from the young girl. The child played by herself every day, and this did not escape my young mother's notice.

Feeling for her plight, my mother started playing with her, a little at a time, which was all it took. In no time, my mother became ill and went into the san. She stayed about a year and came out in pretty good shape, and she stayed healthy for a while, but she had clearly been weakened.

Eventually, she got sick again as a teenager and went back in. Her second tour overlapped my father's stay by about six months; she got out first, but during that time my father pursued my mother somewhat relentlessly.

She wasn't really interested at first—who knew why, maybe she herself didn't—and she was slow to warm up to him, and when she left the san for good, she was pretty sure it was all over. But her mother had liked my father when she had met him, and she also had some level of influence upon my mother. When my father was released, he continued to ask her out and she eventually relented. My father's illness did not alter any ambition he had, just the path. My mother saw that they could perhaps build a life together after all, better than the one either of them currently had, and it was not ever rendered entirely clear if my mother had any exposure to my father's alcohol-related, self-medication technique in those early years or not, but they were off and running. Courtesy of tuberculosis.

Fortunately, or unfortunately, for her, she did not know my father before he got ill and went away. Preceding his tenure at the san, when he initially got sick, so, ironically, did his father for a while, both being hospitalized together for a short period of time, though that provided no opportunity for the two of them to connect in any way—too much violence had occurred over too many years. My grandfather was released first, my father remaining through Christmas, leaving him with a most lasting yuletide memory of being hospitalized during a blizzard, preventing anyone, including his mother and father, from visiting him, the squeaky-wheeled sound of dead bodies being whisked away on gurneys during the quiet, sterile Christmas being the only holiday carols, of sorts, for him to hear. And this, quite thoroughly, explains his deep indifference toward the holiday, in stark contrast to my mother's most jubilant December spirit, never otherwise showcased across any other pages of the calendar, though I do give my father lots of credit for remarkably never letting his hospital-experience-tainted holiday sensibility interfere with our household Christmases over so many years. Or extinguish my mother's holiday form of escape either.

Might have been easier to despise him unconditionally had he been passed out shamelessly under a toppled Douglas fir, sprawled across colorful, crushed glass ornaments and the sad remains of GI Joe's, Hot Wheels, and Lite-Brites, so merrily displayed in vodka-soaked, festive, seasonal wrap. But he did no such thing, though a heightened sense of doom every time the advent calendar doors opened closer and closer to the twenty-fifth continued to perplexingly contribute to the mystery and conundrum of just what eventually would trigger his rage, once another merry season would approach then pass without incident.

Perhaps that's why my mother displayed so much December happiness, she had enough history with him to know that this was the only safe season, never having witnessed the damage done to his holiday psyche so much earlier. Little, if any, clues had been available to her. Outside of the san, the only part of his life she saw was that unwavering ambition and his ability to hold a job and be damn good at it.

My father had started working for the Illinois Central Railroad, alongside his father, before he got sick. Once he was finally as healthy as he would ever be, given his years of debilitation, he had no other choice but to continue with the IC to resume job security enough to marry my mother, which he most determinedly did. Past engineering dreams now dashed, though one thing would shortly lead to another, he was nonetheless quite good with numbers at the railroad, and eventually the traffic department at a multi-national firm was interested in hiring him based on how well he handled their rail shipping requirements.

Against everyone's wishes, including that of his beloved mother, and with a young family now in tow, he took the risk, and the job in hometown Chicago, coincidentally one month after I was born. After staying with it for about nine years, corporate headquarters then called and whisked us (oh, so merrily!) away to greater, greener, eastern pastures, and thus, my path to Hamden, and my father's hope for a genetically shared, mathematical continuity had begun. But first, my parents must find a house.

I am sixteen years old and cutting the front lawn of our Eden Falls, white clapboard, two story, colonial house, which sits atop a rolling front yard containing a very big-ass rock with drilled holes for dynamite to blow it away, which was started but never finished, and which pushes up out of the corner of the yard, practically hiding the garage. I gotta hand it to my mother. Months before we were all on our way east for the big move, she and my father went out alone to buy a house, and she convinced him to buy this one. The builder had gone broke, so the house was a bit ... undone shall we say: no painted rooms, no landscaping to be heard of (as far from any Dutch onion field as a lawn could look), and not attracting much attention, especially with the Rock of Gibraltar in plain sight, daring anyone to buy this mess. But it was the most affordable, if you didn't mind eating spaghetti every night, located on a cul-de-sac in a pretty good neighborhood, and reasonably close to Eden Falls Elementary school, where the Jesse's and Norman's of this brave, new world would convince me, however temporarily, that, yes, this move might not be so bad, after all.

My father, on the other drink-toting hand, preferred a house in a different school district in Eden Falls, a bit more sophisticated, and set on a well-respected street that was considered the more "established" part of town. But said street was a winding nightmare to drive, with absolutely no hope of riding bikes on it at all, or of crossing it to run over to a neighborhood kid's house, so we would be stuck on our own newly privileged island, which was not a good option for any of us, especially my mother. She would be the one having to regularly navigate the twisty, turny, woody street on a fairly regular basis (most notably to get to the nearest liquor store to keep the vodka flow uninterrupted) with no next-door neighbor available to watch the kids, so my father gave in and bowed down to my mother's recommendation. And we settled into the Big Rock House with the far-reaching front lawn of flimsy, few and far between blades of grass; my new lawn-cutting chore laid out in front of me now, once there was more grass than dirt to cut so when I finished the job I wouldn't look like Lawrence of Arabia after he crossed the Sinai.

One hazy, hot, summer Saturday, after I got my driver's license, I was finishing up at the farthest end of the lawn when my mother came out of the house, walking directly toward me in a most determined fashion, which sent off red flags everywhere. Not because she was approaching me while I was working on the lawn, but because she was approaching me empty-handed: no cool drink, snack, or nervous, concerned attempt to get me to take a break from the hot sun, and the Pounders-like cloud of perpetual dust hovering around both me and the old, red, noisy Toro lawn mower we brought from Illinois (as if the presence of Midwestern machinery would miraculously coax the best possible growth out of the ubiquitous, rocky, and skimpy East Coast soil my father insisted I get to know quite intimately through lawn mowing, grass planting, weeding, fertilizing, and watering, not to mention digging a six-foot long trough to move a bunch of already rooted bushes, though his, "Ah forget it, it'll probably kill 'em, just fill the hole back up," kind of orders only added to all my other Saturday afternoon, summer scutwork).

I watched my mother approaching across the lawn and I stopped the Toro. I wiped my forehead and caught my breath, knowing this was not the usual visit. Her stride and sorrowful face came into view as she got closer, and I saw her again at the top of the old stairs in West Holland Heights, a record raised defiantly once more above her head. She had been crying and she looked at me and said, while employing my first name very directly, which sent immediate shivers up my back, "Ogden, can you drive me back to Illinois?"

During that moment of instant, eternal silence that so painfully followed her question, the hush on the lawn was overwhelming, perhaps exaggerated by the sudden deadening of the lawn mower engine, its rugged growl so comfortable and so much a part of the weekend auditory experience on the front lawn that its abrupt, awkward silence was too unnatural to endure. I still recall the ironically concurrent atmospheric sounds that surrounded our vacuum of stillness and hung heavy as the humid air during the time between her question and my answer: a blue jay calling from a nearby oak branch, a distant dog bark, a bunch of younger neighborhood kids calling out and accusing each other of some sort of unfairness in a game they must've been playing that was anything but the glorious ones from my preferred Illinois childhood.

A car then passed down the road, the sky yawned with the sound of a jet overhead, and I ended our personal quiescence, all along my head spinning to process my answer, which circled back to vodka, an explosive temper not to be poked, and the potential for greater unknown disaster should I actually abandon the lawn mower right on the spot and retrace the 900 miles back to Illinois, my mother in tow (leaving the Toro as a sort of final artifact or monument to be discovered, a reminder of the death of a family on their way up, and on their way down).

I just looked at her, conflicted, without even knowing what brought this request on, but not needing to know, fully aware that these storms blow in from time to time, great gusts, without forewarning, though we know the pressure is always building. And they do blow in, and we're once again never the same, and we never talk about why Johnny Mathis gets hurled down a flight of stairs, or why we can continue to just go on again when the skies momentarily clear. Yet the immense courage it must have taken my mother to decide to put her teenage son, and herself, at risk because she had absolutely no other option to exit this world showed just how desperate she was. This time.

Oh, the desperation in my perpetually sad mother, and the confusion in how to emotionally decide what was best—she must have needed to get out—but I needed her too. In perhaps the boldest statement I ever made, complete with the most agonizing sorrow and pain I could imagine at that instant, I looked into her unrealistically hopeful eyes, for only a moment, then looked down at my shoes and said, with incongruous resolution, "I can't, Mom."

She said nothing, knowing all along, I'm quite sure, that I could not honor this request for the devastation that would ensue from my father. Knowing I knew this as well, she turned away, this moment of silence perhaps even more devastating because I remember no other ambient sounds at all at that point, just the sound of a world gone silent in a moment of embarrassing respect for what was surely the passing of some great and final hope that we might at last be allies, the way my father and grandmother out of similar necessity once became.

She headed back to the house, the growing distance between us and the lack of any further words a clear acknowledgement that we both knew her request couldn't have been fulfilled; we both knew that we both knew this; we both knew why, and we also knew we were aware that we were sharing the same prison cell and would continue to do so.

Not that either one of us could ever save the other, despite the presence of at least one adult at any given point in time, but, in the oddly (and momentarily) peaceful acknowledgment of the personal defeat we now most shamefully shared, we absolutely knew that she was unable to forgive herself for getting me into this, and I was unable to forgive myself for not being able to get her out.

I turned toward the Toro and pulled the cord, and it started up right away, loud, strong, and purposeful. I finished the lawn, going over and over it before returning to the house my mother chose for our future, making sure not a single blade of grass was overlooked, standing falsely tall, hopelessly out of place.

I like grass. I like the solitude of cutting grass, being all alone, following a mostly mechanical process requiring no real concentration, except when you clear the clumps from the blade underneath so as not to cut your hand off, but other than that you can get lost in the process, and I like getting lost. Still.

And I liked to walk home from Hamden, too, to brood and ponder things uninterruptedly, like grass, and how its presence underfoot, and things that happens upon it, can change every-thing. I could easily get lost in thought, with undisturbed regularity, whether mowing our lawn or walking home among the far-reaching yards of the wealthy, breathing in someone else's freshly cut, onion-free grass, the difference being that the lawns I walked by near Hamden were all mowed during the day by gardeners, not in the evening by fathers coming home from work, or by me on Saturdays. So, I got the benefit of the sweet, aromatic bouquet at daytime, connecting me oddly to West Holland Heights every time I breathed it in, and not, thankfully, to the hot, dusty grass of a sorrowful mother's approach. Or the evening, dewy grass of an open field and an upcoming, different kind of experience altogether, still fresh in my mind.

And it seems most unfortunate, and a bit cruel as well, that something as harmless as grass can captivate you early on in your life, with sweet smells and lasting images that even a stray bit of onion here and there can't spoil. But just when you let your guard down, and you're pretty sure you can lie down safely in green pastures beside Biblically still waters, those same verdant fields become more like minefields, and the water like rapids, and this is the kind of thing worth pondering when you are all alone and walking home.

It was a good forty-five-minute walk from Hamden to my house, plenty of time to perambulate such lush perimeters pensively on any given late afternoon until you hit familiar landmarks such as the house of one of my, thankfully, non-prep school friends—a girl named Kylie. She was one of about seven teenage kids I hung around with outside of school, and they all lived either on my street or close by, some of whom I knew from all the way back at Eden Falls Elementary school, all of whom I was so much more comfortable with than anyone at Hamden. I never saw any of my Hamden class-mates, interestingly enough, anywhere in Eden Falls outside of

school, making it quite easy to carry around two different personas with me at all times–one clearly more relaxed than the
other–and to deploy each effortlessly, with absolutely no risk
of any awkward commingling whatsoever. And that's exactly
what I did.

But I may have lied, just a tad, about Hamden being my
only exposure to kids from different countries. Kylie was from
Australia and her family was in Eden Falls on some business
assignment. They had lots of international friends and while
one might think that to be quite the worldly exposure, having
a connection to any country outside my own only conjured up
lasting images of my experience with Chloe, and her eventually heading overseas, which did not encourage me in any way
to embrace a sensibility for welcoming the world at large with
open arms.

So, of course, that very same early summer when Chloe
left, and while I was still processing the experience of a first
girlfriend, of sorts, over and over again, excogitating the whole
episode thoroughly, over and over again, Kylie had a foreign
houseguest: Nathalie Lefebvre from France. And just like that
I was back on quite uncomfortable turf.

While it was quite magical for most of the guys in our group
to have a bombshell like Nathalie dropped on our neighborhood doorstep one early June evening, I wanted no part of it.
None of us had any idea why Nathalie was there, when exactly
she was leaving, and why this happened only once. We never
heard of her or saw her before, never heard from her or saw her
again afterwards, and this attribute of suddenly appearing and
disappearing seemed to be quite common in my experiences
with seductively stunning, summery girls passing through
Eden Falls right around the end of the Vietnam conflict, their
enticing, feminine, regional speech patterns fully on display.

While Chloe had a bit more of a, shall we say, charming
Southern enunciation, Nathalie spoke most heart-stoppingly

avec un accent français authentique–quite the irresistible, auditory splendor! It could have easily been reason enough to reconsider my self-evaluation, surrender my kneecaps most wholeheartedly to Kylie's gravel driveway (complete with occasional shards of camouflaged, broken glass), and most humbly thank the stars above for an opportunity to right all wrongs and try, yet again, to be someone other than the real me. Especially since Nathalie's introductory pronunciation was astoundingly further enhanced, if that was even possible, by the presence of a non-participatory voiceless-vowel-consonant in her first name. Exactly like Chloe! Who knew a silent 'h' could carry such weight, and appear twice in my, however hesitant (though nonetheless heated), horny hijinks, and in the same summer, no less!

But it instantly occurred to me that this uncanny carbon copy of a possible, summer romance scenario, ratcheted up a notch by unfairly throwing France into the mix, was either a test of my conviction in my own new, sad-sack, self-discovery, or some colossally cruel mishap occurring because someone in the heavens above got distracted when my DNA map was next in line for a healthy sprinkling of age-appropriate, sexually charged, developmental genes.

Either way, I was convinced that I would not by any means 'change' (grow, move on, let go, embrace, etcetera) so soon after Chloe had left (and while the vodka king's influence was still sadly hanging overhead), so the ultimate outcome of my adolescent, summer, sexual development was at the mercy of the same social construct just as punishingly laid out as that of my Hamden experience: involvement with those vastly ahead of me, and to whom I prohibited myself from ever catching up.

I was determined to keep my distance from Nathalie in order to completely avoid another Chloe-like, open field mishap. But also, to sidestep any encounter whatsoever with any girl who was going to see me for who I was, so quickly after one already had, and who would reconfirm what Chloe already knew about me, thereby allowing my most preferably hidden features to slowly creep into the public domain, courtesy now of two initially interested, but alarmingly frustrated females. And there's no emotional copyright law in the land that would protect me from that disaster. Besides, dammit, it would only most likely have made me realize just how extraordinary Chloe might very well have been. I didn't want to know that yet.

I was fairly certain, though, that there would be no connection to worry about with Nathalie. This was not going to be a case of letting my guard down on a humid, summer evening back porch, like with Chloe. No, no, no, my guard was up and on call, and there would be absolutely no surprise, witty comments to turn any heads my way, no matter how blonde and stereotypically gorgeous. And I, in no way, was going to perseverate over yet another marvelously silent 'h' (however fetchingly French), which could have easily given rise to some slippery comment sneaking through that might have unwittingly caused her to toss that wild mane back and throw open that delightfully delicious mouth of hers, emitting that most glorious French-tinted laugh. No, no, no! Chloe was a first for me and, as I said, I didn't want another first girlfriend, or even another idea of one, because that might have taken me far longer than originally thought to finally decide whether or not to love Chloe retroactively, and I didn't want anything to interfere with that long and detailed process. Plus, I just couldn't do that to a Southern girl in absentia whom I would never see again—they're the most important girls in your life.

As much as I had always passed Kylie's place on my walks home, I had never been inside her house before Nathalie's arrival, or since. But all us guys spent more time there that summer than anywhere else, though that was not at all my idea. That first evening that we stopped by to pick Kylie up to go somewhere forgettable, I'm sure, Nathalie appeared with her at the back screen door, maniacal blonde hair, flowing summery skirt, slightly limited English (though overwhelmingly preferable to Jesse Pelagatti's earliest version), and there was nothing I could have done if I wanted to continue seeing my friends other than to keep coming back with them. Which Kylie picked up on right away, curiously dangling the desirable Nathalie in front of our group's largely slobbering, summertime, sexual energy to ensure our continued visits in much the same way she lured away from company with a distracting treat, especially after a dinner of uncertain and highly combustible (though apparently quite tasty) contents, her beastly, breathy pet Beagle, not so affectionately nicknamed 'Gusty' for his distinctly (and quite ever present) gale-force, belching capabilities.

Most calamitously, it appeared Nathalie liked me, dammit, despite my best withdrawal efforts, though I was never very good at knowing these things for sure, and I was, as I said, especially leery after my experience with Chloe. But I had a hunch I was right about her intentions when she strategically placed her left breast into my opened hand one particularly humid, though breezy, early evening while at Kylie's house yet again, no plans to speak of, just hanging out in her room, allowed by her mother if we kept the door wide open.

Nathalie was lying down on one of the two beds when we came in, Kylie was on the other, and the rest of us sat on the floor, most of us full of energy, all of us aimless and antsy. I somehow frighteningly ended up near Nathalie.

For unquestionably obvious reasons, a window had already been mercifully thrown wide open in the event of Gusty's aromatic arrival; for some unexplained reason my hand was wide open as well—think we were all comparing our life and love lines, or something stupid like that.

Nathalie, quite unannounced, lurched suddenly and reached out to grab something falling off the nightstand, though I don't remember anything falling off at all, and in the process, her left breast landed firmly, squarely, and, without hesitation or concern, directly into my opened palm. She then rolled over slightly, pressing it in place long enough until it would stick, most determinedly, as if she were using Elmer's glue on a school science project.

Nobody saw or said anything; it happened too fast and surprisingly naturally (for her, not me—this was my first independently copped feel not requiring any preplanning or active participation on my part whatsoever). There was also no recoil from her, no embarrassment displayed anywhere in the room, no awkward laughter, or even jealousy on anyone's part, though I was sure my jackrabbit heartbeat, however alarmingly continuous, even well past its understandably jittery jump start, would be loud enough to summon Kylie's mom to come running. But it happened under everyone's radar; no parents appeared in any doorway, and there I was, stuck in a timeless, nervous second that lasted as long as a chance encounter in a Hamden stairwell, the surprised recipient of an errant, French tit. Nothing to do now but sit among friends and wait for it to eventually find its way out, like a bird trapped in a garage. And, much to my relief, it did, before anyone was the wiser, except for Nathalie, and me, though when she rolled back over to reassemble her ample charms, it was as if nothing had happened and, I can't deny it, how savvy and sophisticated are the French. Even though my overworked nervous system begged me to reconsider, quite emphatically, mind you, convincing me to wait for its twin to swoop in next, quite certain that breasts, like neighborhood nuns, prefer to travel in twos, I remained steadfast, and the additional, AWOL appetizer never appeared.

Thankfully. You can live in desperate attempts at denial for only so long. Phantom items falling off nightstands are fine rationalizations if you're never going to allow yourself to admit that the real reason you can't enjoy a bird in the hand, so to speak, is because you're still convinced that any ornithological, bosomy enticements still had to come from Chloe. And that was a kind of betrayal that my fluttering heart and nervous stomach, most decidedly, confirmed.

I, in no way, would have ever expected to have been chosen by someone so desirable across two continents, simultaneously, as Nathalie Lefebvre, and be the envy of my non-prep school, self-proclaimed, Francophile buddies as well, even had I been in a position to wholeheartedly embrace the advances of our new French toast of the town. As intriguing as she was, it would have been much easier, for me, to have imagined her beauty in a monumental, masturbatory, Keegler-master-bedroom-inspired mania instead, where I could've applied my recently honed skills, courtesy of Chloe, instead of venturing into any unbridled, hot romances where French pastries might show up in either hand at a moment's notice, and without forewarning.

Especially as it became clearer that by preferring me, Nathalie was bypassing the very sexually charged, worldly, and most attractive of us guys to the girls: Jason Murell, who looked enough like Jagger (including hair) to make any girl instantly swoony and every guy hopelessly pissed off and jealous of the attention and forthcoming stories of his extracurricular exploits. And I would never have wanted that level of public exposure anyway, even if I had been miraculously granted a new reckless, open-armed, neurological make-up as a gratuitous do-over. No doubt Jason and Nathalie had to happen—it only made sense—and, admittedly, would have made most of us exhale anyway, certainly me, with the knowledge that that is indeed the way the world always works, the rest of us can only dream, once again comfortable where someone else has determined we belong.

I didn't know if I would ever be ready to experience that kind of "French Revolution," so to speak, but certainly not at that moment. As I had said, I could not, even if it was possible, risk succeeding with Nathalie in areas that didn't quite pan out with Chloe and that I was still mulling over, by the way, in order to hopefully arrive at some conclusion about myself. That would've totally disrupted the protective sensibility that I had quickly adopted upon Chloe's departure, in order to positively process my experience with her, and how she introduced me to myself, which was not at all her fault but certainly her doing. And I didn't want someone else who was eventually headed home across the same ocean that Chloe had to cross to have the same experience with me as Chloe had, and then perchance run into Chloe in some café where they can be overheard giggling profusely at my expense.

As I said, you want to stay out of the public domain.

It's bad enough if two girls know who you are, but if word gets out beyond them? Well, it's never a good idea to have a highly civilized, foreign citizenry know as much about you as you would prefer to remain unknown. She should have placed her French Pop Tart in Jason's hand, dammit, not mine. I had to continue to stay safe. I had to, while I continued to figure things out. Mostly about Chloe.

Chloe was my first real girlfriend, meaning, unlike Nathalie, someone I might actually become an active participant with, not just the lucky recipient of keenly tossed, upper body parts. And I did become a participant. Sort of. But, to tell you the truth, everything about Chloe was and still is a blur. A lot happened between Chloe and me while at the same time absolutely nothing happened at all. In less than a year, and in no particular order, or with any discernible timeline of events available to my memory even to this day, I met Chloe; she laughed; she talked; I listened; there was a kiss (after the cemetery); it rained; I got my driver's license; South America came to mind; my father continued to drink; I had pizza; my mother tumbled into further mystery; my heart pounded endlessly and entirely without reservation; I quite possibly fell in love; I fell out of a tree; I most assuredly fell in love (with something), and for the most part I was fully and gloriously nauseated from the time I met Chloe until the day she left, especially when it mattered most.

And she did leave. I, sadly, and perhaps (though most likely not) unwittingly, built my first, prophylactically inspired, fence around Chloe, or me, just before she moved away, which was not at all her doing, or the direct result of any regurgitating displays of affection on my part, though an argument could be made against that particular point. No, she was eventually dragged overseas by an oil executive father (surprise!) who was transferred once a year to the latest metropolis located near the next biggest oil glut to exploit, so we poor, preppy saps could wait in endlessly long and orderly gas lines to drive around *les femmes fatales du sud des Etats Unis and la République Française* alike, which is where all similarities between Chloe and Nathalie seem to end. But maybe not.

Chloe was a pretty cute girl, hailing at the time from somewhere unpronounceable in either Texas, Oklahoma, or Louisiana, but definitely connected to the domestic oil reserves far out in the Gulf of Mexico, and coming with the requisite, Southern accent, and a talent for attracting males with every breath she took, arguably unintentional, but certainly, as her favorite President (surprise!) Honest Abe himself would put it, "with malice toward none," and a bit of "charity for all."

So, any parentally fortified bastions to preserve her teenage modesty and accompanying chastity never stood a chance. Not to say her potential proclivities were a problem at all; *au contraire, mes amis,* when all was said and done, I admired Chloe, not so much for her eyes, and her hair, and her nose, and her appreciably minimal, summer wardrobe–those things were all worthy of highly focused and uninterrupted gawking. No, it was her unencumbered spirit (allowing her the full

spectrum of intent behind good ole' Abe's 2nd inaugural address) that I envied beyond anything else. She sure boiled that
speech down to the most basic twentieth-century, adolescent,
hormonal needs, with no anxiety in her to be found anywhere.
And yet she was selective upon her arrival in the neighborhood, seemingly choosing me (not unlike Nathalie did), making
me at first uncharacteristically cool with the idea (not at all
like with Nathalie), and causing me to inch toward her spread-
those-wings-far-and-wide sensibility, most surprisingly.

But ultimately, and in short order, I returned to me as I
always do. But, oh! A girl worldly enough to make my head
spin, if only for a fleeting, sparkling moment, who actually
thinks, no, who knows, she can choose someone, maybe everyone, maybe no one, who cares—it's her decision! And, dammit,
if fate didn't comply, courtesy of the trajectories of our collective fathers, by throwing us sadly, painfully, magnificently,
cruelly, and forever longingly together. Briefly.

I first met Chloe on a hot, summer weeknight, the night
air heavy from the humidity, filling out my rather oblong head
of long, unruly, cool (only to me), and eyebrow-raising (to
everyone else), messy hair with enough unmanageable, though
playfully springy, volume to keep the sweat pouring strategically down my cheeks, in what I alone was convinced was
quite an enticing addition to my otherwise typically wallflower
presence. The same group that would head over to Kylie's on
some future, summer evening to drink in the best of French
female libations was hanging out at another kid's house on our
street, Old Neversink, deep in the most rewarding of seasons:
summer, for being as far away from Hamden as possible.

I headed over on what would otherwise have been a most
boring, typical, and forgettable evening had Chloe Ellen Quinn
not just moved into the neighborhood, had she not been walking her dog down the street and met Kylie and a few others on
the way, had she not been invited to hang out on a back porch,

had she not been wearing cutoff jean shorts, and sitting in a kind of yoga-pose-lotus-position with her legs crossed and appealingly visible, her equally wild though supremely beautiful mess of long, thick, chestnut brown hair as meteorologically-induced as my own.

I walked onto the porch, and I think our hair was the first of our body parts to become kindred, voluminous spirits of sorts, and in deference to the humidity and all the collective, overactive sweat glands pumping at full steam to combat the oppressive night, a certain secretion-related camaraderie was forged amongst us all, allowing Chloe to drink in the group and feel at home, initially, while putting me in a most surprisingly deflated level of anxiety not normally seen in these parts whenever a new female has broached the surface of my most guarded, emotional ocean. This was unheard of behavior on my part, most likely exhibited with no expectation of caution whatsoever, because Chloe, being brand-spanking-new to our neighborhood, was certainly by no means looking for a connection of any kind. She probably still had a boyfriend back home and was wrestling with the new strains of distance, so surely that and the probability of her still being under the influence of jet lag, or central standard time, put my anxiety to bed earlier than usual.

My propensity for total, inward immersion relaxed a bit, and I put my feet up on the railing in a sort of nod of appreciation to the mental health benefits being unwittingly doled out to me through the marvels of modern aviation and time zone demarcation. And then the joke came. And I casually tossed a fall of hair out of my face with the slightest sense of misleading confidence, giving the trickles of sweat their moment to shine. And Chloe laughed and looked my way. And everything changed.

I don't even remember what the line was that prompted my bon mot of sorts, but it spewed forth with a dash of both whimsy and aplomb, pithy, yet decidedly harebrained and proudly empty-headed. Apparently, it was just the right slap-happy cocktail of mirth and merriment the night demanded for Chloe laughed aloud and comfortably, caught off guard in the presence of veritable strangers, not at all self-conscious about feeling too comfortable too soon, and even I could tell that her laugh, and her head-tilt my way were open invitations for me to get to know her better. And I did. Starting at either 9:31 pm, or 10:31pm, depending upon one's preferred choice of time zone, I connected most fatalistically with Chloe on an otherwise meaningless and forgetful August, Wednesday night, courtesy of a surprisingly welcome, lame joke that let my anxiety slip momentarily through the back door like a sneaky cat.

I seemingly let myself go for the first time I could remember that night, despite the ever-present company of my three oldest and dearest friends who always have my best interest at heart, but who were clearly asleep at the wheel that fine night: screaming voice (in my head), rising bile (in my stomach), and draining blood (from my face). Whatever came over me had let everything go for the moment and let Chloe in—a most risky yet alluring arrangement. And so, it began. And my heart and stomach were never the same.

Chloe lived at the end of Old Neversink. With no Hamden Academy in her future since she would be going to Eden Falls High, it was easy for us to begin. She had no connection to anyone even on the outer edges of my life, so any time we met, anything we talked about, it was just us, no common friends quite yet (only back porch acquaintances so far, for her), no brothers or sisters involved, and no parental friendships en-tangling my initially awkward and surely queasy, visible-to-the-general-public-at-large interactions.

So, it was completely uncomplicated to run into her, or stop over at her house, and certainly there was no need to make a big deal out of it or worry about announcing any intentions to anyone. It all started happening within the limited scope of my comfort level of operation and, much to my surprise, a certain level of unfamiliar calmness slowly cozied me up like a cashmere sweater on a winter's night. And I wore that sweater precariously, though intermittently, well, especially in the beginning, and I do think the insulated, womb-like environment of just her and me in the neighborhood was the key to the progress made, along, most assuredly, with her bronze-ish legs and cut-off shorts.

It was a good thing she came along in August and not December, and it was especially a good thing that it was a particularly humid and rainy summer and fall because the rain kept us inside one afternoon when I popped over to her house. We had nothing else to do that day but lie around on the floor, listen to the Moody Blues, and talk under an opened window, and that's when I first got to climb aboard the good ship Chloe, though fully clothed, in an effort to test the boundaries of my untrustworthy, dormant anxiety. Just to see when the crowned, red prince of vodka would rear its ugly head inside my own, of course, and reawaken the nerves that, for the moment, were willing to let me roll as is to see precisely how far I was willing to go. And that approach yielded quite a gem because while I was about to lean in for our first, real deep kiss under a rainy window, I got a pretty good look up her nose—clear as a bell, no pesky, unwanted, nasal cavity whistling, and one nostril shaped like Peru! I loved that! Still do.

When I told her that she had a geographically correct nostril and that maybe she should think about contacting the Guinness Book of World Records, she threw that mess of humid hair back and, with those great green eyes of hers, she laughed. I loved the sound her laugh made while her nose respectfully resembled one of the premier, must-see, cultural, tourist stops of the southern hemisphere! How could you not love a girl like

Chloe? You couldn't, and I was overwhelmed by her reaction, and I hadn't even kissed her yet. But that's when I knew that delightful, facial orifices aside for the moment, I could quite possibly love this girl.

And I was pretty sure I did, right then and there, though you can never be too sure about those things. And you must certainly be on guard should you go ahead with it, of course. And I was.

With an impulse-defying logic, surely attached somehow to my discovery, I inexplicably leapt up and off of Chloe, though regrettably kiss-less for the moment, and suggested we go for a rainy drive, so I could properly contemplate the wonders of her seemingly adenoid-free, unobstructed, Inca-inspired sneezer (an anatomical blessing to be sure, and most assuredly quite unlike my own). She looked at me kind of funny-like, but must have sensed a bit of a madcap, the-hell-with-any-gas-line-Arab-oil-embargo-crisis kind of frisky energy in me, so she quickly took to the idea, liking it more and more as we dashed out the front door into the downpour and raced towards my old Chevy, parked on the street from yet another impulsive move to drive to her house earlier instead of walking, even before the rain had started, and sometimes, like that time, an impulse is all you need to do the right thing. So, off we went, soaking wet and both of us feeling like something fun and exciting could very well happen on such a mindless, drenching afternoon.

We took off aimlessly, no plan in sight, just splashing along the back roads and blasting the radio when Chloe crossed her legs, right over left, and started bouncing that right foot of hers, revealing the taut skin on her most captivating and quite structurally sound ankle, which I found so immensely appealing and certainly a serious contender to dethrone her sub-equatorial nostril as an up-and-coming favorite bodily feature. She bopped that foot up and down with increasing pluck and a devil-may-care attitude that was most certainly due to the freedom customarily afforded by a roomy, private, front car seat, and the lack of a protective, concealing, and often constraining, pair of sanitary ankle socks.

Ah, the Chevy was a good place to be in the rain. It was both insulation and unbridled excitement in motion: leaving someplace, heading toward another, though leaving always stuck with me the most (certainly the more common experience back then, though, admittedly, sometimes the most desirable). We kept driving, me paying more attention to Chloe's uncovered, finely sculpted, bronzed and excitingly skeletally pronounced anklebone than the road ahead when I just happened to look up and notice a cop up there, moving the traffic around. That sure didn't look right. And then I saw why.

"I think we just joined a funeral procession," Chloe said.

Sure enough, the Chevy had cut into the middle of a line of cars being ushered down a hill and through the entrance to Eden Falls Cemetery.

"I don't think we should be here," I said, with great insight, so I did the only thing I could. The road leading to the grave was pretty narrow—I couldn't turn around—so I stopped, breaking the line of cars slowly driving in. Then I did one of those three-point turns that I, thankfully, did pretty well when I passed my driving test, and, before I knew it, I was pulling a U-turn out of the funeral procession and heading back against the wet traffic. The people behind were looking at us flabbergasted, and even the cop at the top of the hill threw his hand up to halt the incoming traffic, utterly astonished. I'm guessing he didn't expect to ever have to do that.

Just as we approached the cop and stopped in front of him until he felt the time was right to stop the flow and let us exit, I intuitively felt compelled to roll down the drippy window and bond with him during our precious, few moments alone, to hopefully stem the rising tide of his disgust toward me. And just in that dead, silent moment when two people look at each other before anyone speaks, and one of them is thinking, 'what is this asshole doing?' while being pelted with droplets thrown from wiper blades unnecessarily positioned on high, an adorably small, audible, and rapid-fire discharge of something like rectal vapor, surprisingly redolent of Monday morning algebra, emitted from Chloe's direction. Insufficiently muffled, I'd like to point out, and forever linking my car and my classroom as unsavory, inanimate soul mates of sorts.

Though her mistimed bombardment was not visible at all, and hardly therapeutic in the least, I nonetheless sprang to her assistance. Uncharacteristically quick on my feet, and, in an effort to distract the cop from the profusion of unsettling emissions clearly headed his way through the opened window, I offered an air-tight explanation for our otherwise uncalled-for exit, "We're still a little bloated from breakfast, officer; it's probably best we depart these most peaceful burial grounds. Now."

Underscored most convincingly by Chloe slinking below view in the passenger seat and assuming the position of the mortified, the displeased and fuming cop immediately, and quite emphatically, waved us through, regardless of the brake lights and tire screeches his effort produced. "Thank you for your service to the freshly embalmed," I said, as reverentially as possible, while waving, quite a departure from my winning way of a few weeks back, seeming now like decades ago. But I suppose the comfort of a late night, humid back porch is generally more conducive to heart-stealing quips than is the confusion surrounding a gaseous, mistaken, cemetery excursion. We headed out.

Once we exited and were safely well on our way along the wet roads, and back to our normal selves (misbehaving, lower portholes thankfully closed tight for the moment), Chloe's flushed cheeks resumed their more familiar, almost caramel-like, glow, and she started to exhale noticeably, employing the use of a much appreciated and far more agreeable, above-the-belt, and splendidly toothy, bodily opening.

"Sometimes that happens when I get a little nervous," she offered, still preoccupied with her most unfortunate and un-appetizing brush with the law.

"I'm so embarrassed!"

"Oh, don't worry about it," I interjected, "I'm sure he didn't notice the stench."

I'm still not too sure that comment entirely helped her, or further endeared me to her, but, damn it, every stupid word I uttered during the whole cemetery scene was just an example of how Chloe could at times bring out the worst in my verbal capabilities. Because girls like her do that to you, once you see how great their ankles and nostrils are, and it's a damn good thing I told her that joke on that back porch before I took in-ventory of her bodily features, both outward and inward facing. But she nonetheless did seem to appreciate that I jumped right in with the cop and offered an explanation most confidently, however half-baked, that included the word 'we' and not just 'she.' I could tell she appreciated the joint ownership of her most regrettable release, and though I had to keep my eyes on the road to avoid inappropriately joining any further, un-welcoming, solemn processions, I could see out of the corner of my eye that she began to relax even more now (perhaps she was thinking of my back porch joke, weighing again the unu-sual benefits awaiting her through a connection with someone possessing, on yet another occasion, both a curious dash of graveyard (in this case) panache, and a healthy sprinkling of barnyard, out-to-lunch, imbecilic, and quite quivery fortitude. Overall, an acquired taste for a select few to appreciate. In this case, one Chloe Ellen Quinn).

Chloe then shifted in her seat, turning slightly toward me, her left leg bent and slightly underneath her now, resting on the seat, as if she was settling in and turning toward me to continue the bonding moment that unplanned, airy funeral processions so freely provide. I liked seeing her leg tucked underneath her like that in a kind of vulnerable, trusting position. Made me feel good, though at times I have to admit that maybe she shouldn't have felt so comfortable around me, given the level of anxiety perpetually lurking around the corner. Maybe it would have been better if she was just a little nervous, giving me a perceived sense of daring and edginess to accompany that confident and take-charge attitude that comes from blindly obeying a cop's directions to proceed headlong through a local community's quite peacefully pleasing gates of eternal rest.

It's not always good to have someone too comfortable around you all the time. I especially wanted her to be at least a little on guard against raging hormones that I know I did not in any way possess but wanted so desperately to believe would intertwine us nonetheless at a moment's notice. I wanted her to be guarded and excited, loins anticipating a mad dash in the rain and impulsive drive to answer the steamy callings of the best, tree-lined, pristinely manicured, two-car-garage-family-oriented neighborhood yards Eden Falls was about to offer us.

Chloe then sat straight back, re-crossed her legs, and started bouncing her foot rhythmically again, slowly at first this time, then gradually picking up speed, treating me yet again to her ankle at work and all the visual joy such synovial hinge-type joints so selflessly provide. She looked pretty content there, and I hoped she would continue to do that for the duration of our drive. And that's when I remembered, years back in Illinois, a bunch of us kids hanging around, doing nothing, when the surprisingly coolest to us (despite his confusing outward appearance) teenager on the street happened to be walking by and, for some unknown reason, he, Gordy Ronkowski, started telling us about girls.

At that moment, watching Chloe bounce her foot, I distinctly remembered the gangly, girthy Gordy telling us how girls masturbated, most commonly by crossing their legs and bouncing the very same foot that Chloe was currently employing with great zeal. The trusted Ronkowski Syndrome! Here in my car! She bounced away, and while I was, of course, entertained each time she performed, I also started wondering just why she chose the worn-out, green, plaid interior of a '64 Chevy as her upholstery of choice upon which to satisfy herself. Sitting right next to me, no less, and having no self-consciousness anymore, or worries about the beast she might unleash in the awkward, skinny, pimply, hairy, anxious driver sitting, oh so close.

It seemed like the longer she took care of her business, the more likely it was that things such as childhood crushing, local-teenager-supplied, introductory sex lessons and the sudden need for absorbent front seat covers might continue to come to my mind to further enrich the experience for me and provide much needed context. I hoped she would keep going, if only to see just what other connections I might be able to contribute. In my enlightenment on the matter, I glanced over one more time and said, "I can move the seat back if you need more room."

Impressive, vehicular, self-entertaining techniques notwithstanding, Chloe required no extra room and looked at me quite confusingly. But she and the rain suddenly lost their respective determination (one perhaps a tad more self-conscious, once again, than the other), both efforts slowing to a trickle then stopping altogether as the car hissed and splashed down the road and Chloe sat in assumed, satisfying silence. We ended up circling back toward her house during our afternoon drive through grief then gas then girlish gratification, and I parked the car on a side street near Old Neversink and right under a tree. We got out to take a walk when, all of a sudden, she grabbed my hand as the rain began again, and we ran back under the tree, and on some unsuspecting neighbor's front lawn I kissed Chloe for the first time, delighted by the fact that the energy so freely disbursed by her ankles just moments ago (and on momentary hiatus along with the rain, Chloe so meteorologically influenceable) had now successfully migrated to her mouth. And she welcomed mine most wholeheartedly, apparently fully on board now with my sensibilities, regardless of any more potential, automotive, detour curveballs I could lob her way should a police officer directing traffic be involved.

In a wet, messy splendor, we kissed on a stranger's most pleasing front lawn, dangerously close to some old bastard surely sitting in his living room watching TV with nothing better to do on a rainy day, having no idea of the comfort and encouragement his freshly cut lawn, and appropriately pruned tree, provided in my endeavor to throw anxiety caution-like to the wind and begin something special with Chloe, in a most fortuitously timed, post-front-car-seat-satisfying moment.

I liked kissing Chloe because she kissed me right back, on her own accord, and I especially liked kissing her during periods of tropical moisture flows lifting from the Gulf and heading our way, much as Chloe herself did from the same region, and I couldn't help but make the connection between the juicy air and her juicy lips. And that most stimulating conflation led me to watch future local weather forecasts much more eagerly, and preferably in private, hoping for a repeat of those most horny, atmospheric conditions so as to reimagine, most self-satisfyingly, and to the fullest extent possible, behind closed, locked doors (and in the same guarded, breathy silence first employed the night after the Keegler, hormonal awakening party), that feeling of water running haphazardly down our pressed-together faces, pooling in areas that would normally allow a runoff were it not for the joy of our combined facial flesh, and putting me in quite a surprisingly poetic mood, the words, the rain upon the lips of leaves coming immediately, and quite enticingly, to mind. And I liked and surely obsessed, for quite some time, over the sound of rain on overhead leaves, and poetic lines needing further development, and the false sensation that those lines protected you from the elements, though, clearly, they didn't, because water, like everything, finds you. Regardless.

But it's nice to think there's always a chance, no matter how remote, that you'll be safe, should you find yourself, for example, falling out of a tree, let's say, and landing spread-eagle onto the hood of your car in yet another inexplicably impulsive effort to impress an all-accepting, albeit very soggy, girl, this time with a fistful of souvenir leaves (lips and all) otherwise out of reach that nevertheless mean the whole damn world to you at that moment. Quite possibly forever.

But you also found that upon hood impact, surprisingly enough, it became instantly apparent that when kissing a rainy girl who was already far ahead of you in self-reliant, carnal car seat skills, well, you had better catch up. And quick. And who knows how much more advanced she could very well be involving others! Shit! I decided I should at least keep up with her personal technique, for starters, and practice on an accelerated basis. I could worry about involving others later. And, hell, if automotive upholstery enabled her craft, then why not enable mine by continuing with cotton, downy pillows! How enticing this connection between us, through the use of fabrics of various texture and time-honored, traditional patterns!

But just when I thought I was making some serious headway against my anxious nature, Bam! It came roaring back when I returned home, soaking wet, from our most unforgettable, drippy outing, and saw empty glasses in the sink, and the ghost of the ruddy, crowned prince of vodka reappearing to me in a most cold-showery fashion, throwing oodles of pounding heartbeats and slow-to-catch breaths my way while at the same time shouting in my ears, "What the hell are you thinking! Do you really want to screw up this once in a lifetime opportunity for your education and become a teenage father working at the car wash the rest of your life?" Respectfully hard-working car washers everywhere notwithstanding, I was apparently groomed to be forever seven years old on a driveway with vodka and a hose, and thoroughly doomed should I even entertain the thought of hosing something, or someone, other than the family Chevy. I guess pillows and poetry precede pregnancy. I was home.

I headed upstairs to wallow in the deepening conflict between excitement for Chloe and the familiar comfort of tyrannical oppression, to see how the two might find common ground to coexist. I couldn't stop thinking about her, and how she inspired me to produce my first poem, however vegetatively themed. I settled on my bed to think about continuing the poem, and I focused on the one thing I felt comfortable with that could keep me connected to her under any circumstances, requiring no additional skills or functionally soft cushioning for assistance. Listening. I liked to listen to Chloe, and talk to her, and I was good at it. My words, at times, would flow off my tongue without seemingly engaging my brain in any preplanning whatsoever. That was certainly dangerous ground, to be sure, and not always confidence boosting, but, often enough, it worked. Nothing earth shattering would be offered, though.

In fact, most of the time, I had no idea what I had just said, or what poetic lines I might now write, but, oh, what joy in discovering something that was just my own! That worked! And as much as I liked to listen and talk to her, I have to admit, I loved that she was saddened by the fact that the other girls in the neighborhood had quickly decided that they didn't really care for her after all, jealous of her charm and country-ish beauty that attracted any male within a country mile, because that gave me the opportunity to be empathetic—a sensibility I didn't know I had but which seemed to be pretty damn effective. And, I have to say, it was considerably genuine and not in the least bit manipulative, which it would have been easy to be under the circumstances.

Which worked quite well for Chloe because she had someone who really listened to her. And it certainly worked exceptionally well for me because you really can't give empathy from a distance, in order for it to succeed there should be little if any breathing room between the two parties. And that capability kept me physically close enough to Chloe so that I could learn first-hand the contours of the upper female body and the never-ending surprise of how breast tapers to waist then waist flows back out to hip. And such a remarkable ebb and flow of the most sensual of tides is so well worth the trip for the unsuspecting hand, upon its maiden voyage, that I continued to purchase return tickets throughout our time together, delaying the trip to points further south. The splendid thigh and all it had to offer at its headwaters, all of it new land yet to be discovered, would have to wait, if it was up to me. It wasn't.

But, like I said, fences were being constructed and, quite frankly, just getting to the point of feeling comfortable north of the border was plenty good from my perspective: really no danger of anything I might be incapable of handling. Fatherhood, on the other hand, was clearly something I couldn't handle. And that was something to really worry about since my first time was coming at me full force now, and with purpose, not unlike one well-intentioned, though grossly off aim, sex manual finding the back of one's unsuspecting head.

No matter how much comfort I found in my occasional ability to give my gift of empathy to Chloe, I was nonetheless intrigued, agitated, and aroused by the inevitable gift of hers I would most likely be receiving, and soon. No matter how much I returned to my bed (over and over) to practice then ponder the conflict of my new state of affairs (over and over), no pillows or positioning, supine or otherwise, upon even the best hypoallergenic, newly introduced, foam supported, cushiony mattress out there held any answers.

Think Chloe pretty much trusted the good guys at the Latex manufacturing plants to apply the latest quality control initiatives to every rubber produced and refrain from the all too tempting desire to goof on any horny adolescent willing to play Russian Roulette with their sorry-ass future, but I, on the other hand, what with so much alcohol ruling our house, couldn't, and wouldn't, take that chance. I sided instead with the all too favorable odds, to me, of some fool spinning the wheel at my expense. Ninety-nine point nine, nine, nine percent is good enough when it comes to pain relief and airline travel, but not good enough when it comes to potential life changing events that would most certainly bring out the wrath of red-white-multi-striped, Russian royalty in our house, and not just on me. One frightening, maternal, wrought iron stairwell incident was enough. But what choice did I have?

Then one evening Chloe and I were making out in her backyard after sharing a most questionable anchovy pizza on her back porch, and amidst all the humidity and cicadas in the trees, the dewy, late night grass, and the beginning of the Watergate scandal, no less, dammit if she doesn't whisper, most encouragingly, and surely to put me at ease about the intended beneficiary here, "I'm ready, Ogden," directly into my ear, thankfully excluding my last name from this much preferred, non-locker room, welcoming gesture. And hearing a girl proclaim her amorous aspirations through direct use of your given Christian name on the cusp of a different kind of historical break-in pretty much clears up any misconceptions floating around out there about the proper, pre-coital protocol to employ during a looming, political crisis. And those three, magnificent, though forever damning, words, "I'm ready, Ogden," riding the humid air upon the magic carpet of her most wonderfully seductive and teasingly anchovy-ed breath, most definitely pulled 'aroused' directly to the front of the line, leaving 'intrigued' and 'agitated' hopefully for another worrisome day.

We immediately headed out of her yard, certain her parents, no matter what room in the house they were in, would smell our hormone soup coming to a boil, as potent now as any startled, summertime skunk in the backyard, and we hurried down Old Neversink, all the way over to the end of Chestnut Ridge and Eden Falls Junior High School. The school field stretched out before us under the blue light of a fat, bright moon. We entered the grass.

"Look how beautiful the moon looks," Chloe said.

"Looks like a Communion wafer," I replied, though I didn't know why I said that. It actually looked more like a Speedy Alka-Seltzer tablet, which I could have used to stem the flow of my nervous stomach acid, now well on its way up the down digestive tract.

But I got lucky, sort of. Chloe liked the Communion wafer comment, and what a great sound her soft, little laugh made in that big, empty, blue-lit field, and I suddenly knew this was it. This was it! My heart rocked and bucked like the Chevy on a cold morning, and I turned to her, swallowing my nerves, my tension, my own doubts and fears, and with a most unfamiliar determination I kissed her in a whole different way. Her breath was warm and alluring enough now, courtesy of that emergency, not yet expired, minimally linty, breath mint called to action from deep within the bowels of her pocketbook, and her skin was, oh! so soft, and we lay down in the cool, wet grass, under the moon, in a place so vast and blue, and we rolled and rubbed and pressed and grabbed and breathed so fast, so heavy, while buttons opened, zippers lowered, clasps broke free, and our hands found new places, softer (softer!) places than could ever be imagined.

My hands raced over Chloe, but were mere tortoises compared to my suddenly hard charging, running-with-the-bulls, kind of mind, and oh, shit! The rubber! Where is it, and where's its companion quality control report? Was the sampling size adequate enough to let mine slip all the way through to production error-free? What if I do something wrong and negate the warranty! There is a warranty, right? What if she still gets pregnant even if I manage to slip it on according to generally accepted, industry standards? I could go to hell!

Hell! Father McCarthy! Our parish priest and pillar of moral guidance! I knew the old bastard would surface out here! Worse yet, what if I like it? What if I like screwing and start thinking about nothing else? What if it messes up my concentration and I fuck up school because I become a teen-aged father! The car wash; the driveway! The vodka king will kill me! And Mom will go over the deep end.

My mind raced through all possible doomsday scenarios, my heart refused to slow down, and my anchovy-heavy stomach rode a tidal wave of nervous acid until I suddenly felt the sweat on my face grow cold—it was so much to take in, too much—and I leapt off of Chloe, yes, I leapt off of Chloe and onto my hands and knees, and, in a further panic, I threw up right then and there under one of the most beautiful moons I had ever seen.

For a moment, it seemed like all time was suspended and I floated right out of my body. I could see, or maybe imagine, Chloe lying alone in the middle of the field. What had I done?

How was I gonna face her?

It seemed like some trick climbing back into my body. There was nothing more I wanted to do than to keep on floating up and away, behind that Communion moon, and away from that whole night, instead of watching Chloe get herself dressed again, feeling kind of alone, I was sure, and walking next to me all the way back to her home. My mouth was so dry and my legs so weak, but my heart began to slow for what felt like the first time since I managed not to barf all over my date.

I still believe that that particular experience was probably not what Chloe had in mind when we left her backyard for a bit of our own space, nor was it an experience to which she was typically accustomed. It was, however, a reaction not without precedent on my part. Who knew open fields and The Lincoln Bedroom could both generate the same reaction from me? And who knew there would be such a connection between Chloe and Honest Abe regarding both wisdom and regurgitation!

But, alas, there would be no boinking the bayou belle during the Nixon years, apparently. Not at all. Chalk it up to a decidedly poor choice of pizza toppings, not an otherwise genuine, however hidden, fear of actually growing up though, right? Right? Regardless, I could exhale; I was safe. In a life I knew how to live, I was once again so very, very safe.

Admittedly, getting the dry pizza-heaves in an intimate moment with your girlfriend could threaten to send the wrong message, but the wrong message was headed her way regardless. Yet a second chance might have been in the making had I completed the embarrassment by instantly rolling my eyes up into the back of my head and hitting the dirt face first, no questions asked, instead of remaining conscious enough to make the kind of choice I did and always do make.

I would like to believe that what happened next was a total reclamation of the person who so freely, if nauseatingly, entered the moonlit field expecting to come out a whole new being. I would like to think that once he regained himself, he returned to Chloe, and I returned to him, climbing back into that awkwardly confused body from that mysterious safe and ghostly place hanging just above it, and from where he and I could both see the whole mess unfurling below without being a part of it.

True, I would have had to then carry that same body around with me for the duration, still without the requisite ten-toe footprint, or proper open-field-teenaged hormonal etiquette, but wouldn't it come in plenty handy when I re-engaged with Chloe? We would go back to making out, letting things go where they were meant to go, from the beginning, and I would go along with it all, and I would be lifted back up to a celestial paradise, but this time with Chloe, all the way to completion, and it would be glorious and relinquishing, and I would make it all the way to a new me–fuck the old me–and when we came back down to earth, I would walk upon it more confidently because I would be different inside. Chloe would not get pregnant due to my steely willingness to fully embrace the Latex manufacturing industry's allowance for up to three standard deviations, and I would not withdraw into any self-manufactured, emotional, safety sheath either. I would be that someone I so desperately hoped I could, at some point in my Hamden-hell of a life, and in my heart of hearts, finally be.

But the night air cooled quickly, and I didn't look at Chloe. She asked me if I was okay, I think, and she somehow managed to gather herself, I think, but I don't recall how that happened, when she stood up, or how embarrassed, humiliated, and or confused she had to have felt when I said nothing and chose not to return to her.

We left the moonlit field as empty as we had found it and walked silently back to her house, my heart frighteningly active, even much more so than when triggered by Nathalie's future wandering breast. I told her I should probably go–I needed to be alone with my palpitations and nerves–and I did, and she went inside, and I didn't know if I could ever see her the same way again because I was certain I would never see me any differently. I suppose I was embarrassed as well, or humiliated, but to tell you the truth, I didn't usually know how either one felt, since those things are remembered as particularly hurtful because they don't come around all that often, so the sting is always fresh. But once you get used to something, there's no sting anymore, just resignation. And that was a pretty damn sad thing to feel, especially on what was ostensibly and otherwise, but for a misguided, queasily defining moment, an altogether considerably delightful, and quite pleasantly fragrant, summerlike evening.

From that point on, surprisingly, Chloe and I managed to work our way through the rest of the school year before she left, though I have to admit my open field maneuvers kind of put a damper on my poetry endeavors. I didn't think I'd ever go back to finishing that poem, though I wrote that first line down on a piece of paper and stuck it in the deep bowels of my wallet, so I'd always have it with me regardless. It seemed like a good thing to carry around with me at all times.

Remarkably, Chloe didn't end our connection. She still liked me listening to her, and she hung on, regardless, in a most sincere (dammit) fashion, until the fossil fuels overseas demanded a drilling of a different sort. When she told me her family was moving at the end of the school year, the first thing that came to mind, considering her being virtual flypaper for all things masculine, was that she was bound to get another boyfriend immediately, so I repressively, and quite easily, rationalized our puzzling relationship away, knowing that I was never the right one for her. She needed someone far more anything than me, and, like I said before, "charity for all", so I figured she'd end up being okay in the oil rich kingdoms that would most eagerly embrace her Lincolnesque sensibility, to the most welcome extent humanly possible, I might add.

I knew she was ultimately confused by the way we kind of drizzled away, not ever taking another stab at a moonlit, open field, but she had to understand that unlike everyone else my age, I couldn't, I just couldn't. Even if we had tried again, it would have never been fully successful ... because, well ... among other things, based on our last experience, I also realized I didn't want her to see my face at the point of rapturous release, when I would have been the most vulnerable and unguarded, not used to throwing caution to the wind when it came to consequences ultimately involving a parent under the influence of ... well ... you know. I may have loved her too much for that, and I didn't know if I could accept anyone I might love seeing me simultaneously spontaneous, ecstatic, and terrified. And I could never have told her that.

I did, however, along the way, tell her a little about the vodka, our move from the comfy Midwest, Hamden, a few things about my mother, and pretty much anything else I could think of that I felt I owed her, in an effort to indeed reclaim a little of myself and transfer any and all moonlit humiliation from her back to me, where it rightfully belonged, but also so that I might feel a fresh new sting, just ... just to feel.

But as much as I truly wanted to give her something of emotional value, I ashamedly had to admit to myself that I was initially somewhat surprisingly relieved that she was leaving, so as not to relive any more open field mishaps, for sure, but, more honestly, I wanted her to confiscate what knowledge of me she currently had and take it far away, over oceans and deserts and mountains, so that I would not see someone, probably ever again, who knew as much of me as I was not yet comfortable with them knowing.

And I wouldn't have to hold my breath while she processed what she knew about me in order to decide whether or not to continue together—and she would decide because, like I had said, she alone can choose what to do with her life and take the consequences herself. And while I could definitely live with a decision of hers, even if it was to part ways (I gotta admit, despite her sticking around I do think she had her fill of me toward the end—who wouldn't), it would hurt far too much just watching her have the internal freedom to decide something for herself. That's a sting I still know best. Regardless of any resignation.

I was not at all sure I did the right thing by telling her everything I did, though. I had grown quite miserably comfortable in my secretive existence at Hamden, and, again, with Chloe being out of the country I could safely return to me, behind my fence, deep in the cave of my own comfort level, and I could get through my days in the ways to which I had grown accustomed, especially with only another two years left before I'd be out of Hamden for good.

So, you would think it was okay to tell her so much. Yet once I did, I wanted it all back. Hearing the words come out of my mouth was not at all cathartic, or enlightening, and it doesn't always feel so good to do the right thing and give somebody something they deserve at great personal cost once you've had some time to reconsider what you've just done. And, quite frankly, I am still not too surprised that I did not particularly feel at all like a new or better person after telling her everything. There's nothing better to be gained from what you know you always are. And, dammit, I hate it when you very well may love someone enough to give them something the deserve but wish you hadn't. And then are willing to let them go.

I took the Chevy over to Chloe's house on the day she left, and I pulled up the driveway, the moving van long since gone. The house looked really weird. You could tell it was empty. I got out of the car. Stay steady, I kept saying to myself, you never know what could happen, and I did, steady as can be, as I walked past her garage. I stopped and peered in. Empty, all right, no cars, no lawn mowers, no hanging ladders, trash cans, hoses (yikes!), all those things that tell you there's a lot of chores to be done so somebody's gotta be there for a long time to do them. Nope, garage was ready for the next family.

I took a deep breath and walked up the walkway to the front door. It was open, and it was so strange hearing the voices of the whole family together: Mrs. Quinn, Mr. Quinn, whom I hardly ever saw, her sisters–both of them, never usually around–and Chloe, the family just milling about waiting for a car to come and sweep them all up and remove the last trace of life from their house, and a tiny Chloe-part from my soul. I walked up the front stairs and rang the doorbell. It practically echoed through the whole, empty house.

"Hi, Ogden," Chloe said, once again making it quite clear by name who the intended beneficiary was (I do love the way she clarifies beneficiaries). I looked at her through the opened door to let her voice roll around in my head one last time. Memorize it. Memmm-or-ize it. When all is said and done, everyone really should have his or her voice remembered. It does make a difference (it would have, Grandfather).

I had to find that place in my head to store the way she says my name, with the e in Ogden that starts out sounding like an a but ends up coming back around, said so quickly you can hardly tell, unless you listen to her. Like I do. I hear every little thing she says. I hear the Hi when you first meet her that starts out being Ha but she catches herself and throws that i on the end at the last possible second. I love when she catches herself! She doesn't know she does it, but she does. And what about Bye? That's my all-time favorite. You'd think it would be like her Hi, starting with that a and ending up with that familiar i. You'd expect it, but–and this is why it's my favorite–she changes it! Rolls it around like it's gonna be a Bi-eee, but she cuts all the e's off, sweeps them up and away to some distant place before they can make it from her tongue to your ear.

Her tongue; my ear. What a great thought! And what about her toes? I don't know what they look like! I told her about mine. Shit, how could I have forgotten that? Are all ten of hers obeying the laws of gravity, and is any particular toe longer than the other? What about the nails? Are they curled, do they fan out, or do they shoot straight out from the skin? For a guy who accurately identified her Peru nostril and internalized every nuance of her voice, I failed her everywhere below the waist, didn't I? And I mean, everywhere.

Except for her ankles. Helluva time to discover that!

While preoccupied with her ignored, various and sundry, lower body parts, I didn't immediately notice Chloe had her purse hanging from her shoulder, her hair finely brushed, make-up on, which she never needed to wear, and hardly ever did, and a coat slung across her arm. I took one look at that coat, heavier than needed for here, and my heart dove down to the bottom of my shoes. I shook off a quick chill.

That coat. She needs it … for when she gets off the plane … somewhere so far away. I wasn't prepared to be knocked off my feet by a dark green coat. I stared at the thing. But I managed to go inside the house. Everyone else scattered off somewhere, giving us our moment of privacy, and Chloe and I stood alone in the hall, right next to the empty living room and right over her basement. The whole house was so empty. So was I. But I held on, held on steadfast as neither Chloe nor I suddenly and awkwardly knew what to say to each other. Almost like our first dance in her basement, directly below where we were standing.

As much as I was a pretty good athlete, I was the most alarming dancer one could imagine. Thanks to my left foot, wayward, little toe I presented quite troubling dance moves.

Beyond comprehension, however, the toe had no effect on my athletic pursuits. I was fortunately most lithe and limber when it came to sports, able to move freely in any direction on a baseball or football field, holding astounding balance while fully comfortable making jaw dropping plays as easily as routine ones. Yet none of that transferred successfully to a dance floor, be it carpeted, linoleum, concrete, or stylishly hardwood.

Textured or waxed, it didn't matter. When I didn't have an independent object around, however small, round or oblong, buoyant or bouncy, to focus on and apply my bodily mechanics without thinking, I did not know how to successfully move my body. Music was just too abstract a thing to motivate any rhythmically compatible movement in me whatsoever, which I discovered at a most inopportune time.

I had figured I would be a natural and could keep up with Chloe, who was somewhat unstoppable, not so much with grace and beauty, but with unbridled energy and fluid motion, and it was highly enticing to watch her throw around assorted limbs and other bodily protrusions, a rope of hair as well, with remarkable timing and rhythm. So, I was actually quite content to just watch her skin paste up with sweat while she moved.

Even though she could dance alone as well as with a partner, I nonchalantly, and quite mistakenly, ambled up to her while the stereo blasted during one musical evening at her house, overcome with the music and the moment, thinking this would be a breeze. She was in full form, and I proceeded to join the frolic on the floor when, as I started, it became quite painfully obvious that I had no idea what to do. I couldn't back out, so I had to think and boogie simultaneously, a fresh, new, cerebral calling. I wasn't used to that. Much to my surprise, while nine grounded toes can get the job done admirably on an athletic field where play eventually starts and stops and offers the opportunity to regroup, that wasn't nearly enough phalanges to ensure the uninterrupted level of balance required for our private, hormonal hoedown.

I immediately, upon movement, listed to the left with no little toe to help curtail the momentum. I then had to jerk responsibly to the right to offset any unintended collision with Chloe, who was mindlessly lost in the music, thankfully. Though my dancing instincts were not in the least helpful, I had to employ them nonetheless in desperate emergency fashion to avoid an out of cadence catastrophe, however catchy and melodious the musical accompaniment.

I thought I could do so by counterbalancing with my arms, reaching to the right as if pulling a tug-of-war rope while teetering left, though this was highly misguided logic. Rhythmic squat thrusts and lunges did no better, and the end result, resembling nothing at all recognizable, seemingly being performed upon a bed of hot coals, no less, was and still is choreography yet to find a permanent home.

Remarkably, I did not crash to the floor, and while oblivious enough to the obvious, I incorrectly assumed these unproven moves might actually be working in harmony with Sly and the Family Stone nonetheless, the music blasting through Chloe's basement speakers in a most encouraging fashion. But I sensed it might be time to wrap it up anyway, wondering just how to end it smartly and crisply, when the music suddenly stopped, and I stomped a foot down to catch up to Sly, my effort a good stride longer, and the force harder and louder than it needed to be, however, and it's fair to say I may have misfired grossly in my timing with the closing of, "I Want to Take You Higher."

In the stunning silence and refreshingly grandfather-less, slaughter-free ambiance of her much-preferred basement, and noticeably long after the song concluded, Chloe took me by the hand. I guess she had noticed my dancing, despite being so personally lost in the music, and she enthusiastically, however awkwardly and kind-heartedly, offered me encouragement, though not so much to trip any more lights fantastic. "I see you've bowled before," she offered up in a most desperate and gallant effort to avoid embarrassing me, or hurting my feelings, while also safely redirecting me back to the comfort of the sporting world, to which she had immediately categorized my dance moves, most understandably.

I guess I didn't have to be so self-conscious about my dancing after all because in the now quiet dampness she also said she had a secret to tell me. And when a sweaty, heavy-breathing girl who has just completed a vigorous cardio work-out is going to tell you a secret about herself, you can bet it'll be a good one.

"It really turns me on when you watch me dance," she tried, again, so very empathetically, "from way over there."

Chloe pointed to a cobwebbed corner of the basement sporting fresh roach bait and a highly visible mousetrap. She then flipped the record over and started up again. I headed over to the banished corner with the attempted swagger of an unrecognized and false victory, all my own, because Chloe felt she could reveal something so personal about herself. To me. Not many girls would be secure enough in their relationship to let a guy know that the farther away he moves from them the hornier they get.

I settled into my new vantage point, content to watch Chloe dance in yet another of her solitary, self-satisfying activities she seemed to prefer whenever I was nearby, while at the same time remaining careful not to disturb the rodent control process Mr. Quinn had recently found so necessary to deploy. Thinking about it now, though, I kind of wish that when Chloe flipped over that record that night, maybe we could have flipped that whole evening over. A lot of evenings with Chloe.

"Ogden, are you okay?"

I hate when empty-house-preoccupied-trances are exposed and you shockingly find yourself back in the present, especially a present so painful.

"I like the way you dance," I mumbled to myself in the empty hallway.

Chloe and I kind of stumbled around each other, trying to laugh a little at my, seemingly to her, out-of-the-blue response, though there was nothing out-of-the-blue about it—again, that's just what she does to me. Then we walked into the living room, which I hated because I saw that window she and I were once under during a rainstorm, and it looked pretty meaning-less now, and perish the thought, like the garage: ready for someone else.

We kept avoiding good-bye right up until the long, black car appeared on the street and pulled up the driveway and Mr. Quinn emerged from a back room and said, "Well ..." Which was all he needed to say. The rest of the family went out to the car ahead of Chloe, and I leaned over, and I kissed Chloe on the lips, and I held it there in one, last, gallant try to mix in with the softness of her mouth and her bitter-tasting, travel-prompted lip gloss, and I breathed in deep and just long enough so I might remember how a girl named Chloe Ellen Quinn tasted and smelled in an empty room the day she had to go. And she did go. With a hand to her cheek and her head hanging down in the back seat of the car, she looked back just once as the vehicle pulled her away from me. But not before she had said to me in that empty room before she left to join her family, "It'll be okay, Ogden, that's what parents do, they plan your life, so you won't relive theirs."

The black car left before I did, and I was supposed to go straight home, but I followed it instead, far enough behind so that I'm still sure she didn't know, and so I could more thoroughly consider her last words to me. I pulled over and stopped to watch from the exit four overpass, as the black bullet exited off Indian Rock Road and onto the turnpike to-ward Kennedy airport. I watched until the speedy, dark speck became one with the moving ribbon of traffic and lost itself, the last raindrop running down Chloe's window.

I stayed there so that at the precise moment when I lost sight of her forever, I could recall how I was truly soaring when our lips met amidst all that water under that rainy tree, so seemingly long ago. And how I was transformed, most assuredly, for the holiest of moments, with a first taste of what it might be like should I be willing to let go of everything I didn't fully understand that defined me and let go in such a way that would surely have lasting consequences. And yes. I kissed the girl in an open field, too, with sincere intent, however shambolic the fizzling mess became. And I would do it again, in the hope that I might soar away forever, if not with her then at least on my own because of her, knowing that I did not have to ever again, in any way, return to me. And I was wrong to process Chloe's leaving through rationalization and guarded relief. Oh, I was wrong! I should have let her departure incite a whole new flavor of anxiety in me, unrelated to alcohol and fathers and mothers, to feel for once the fear of losing something that was all my own, not something that I mysteriously and embarrassingly embodied and obeyed, with overwhelming expectations and duty, courtesy of one parent's immense baggage tossed my way without my permission.

It's like Chloe said, "they plan your life," and hearing somebody say that out loud, confirming what you so desperately needed to keep hidden if you had any hope of rendering it untrue at some point in your life, pretty much convinced me that I would indeed at least love the idea of Chloe Quinn, perhaps much more than Chloe herself. And do so to the fullest of my heart's content. The moment she was out of sight and gone for good.

I needed to love her somehow, and this approach was best because I would never have to look directly into the eyes of someone who told me my life was planned, that I act a little too pretentiously at times, and tend to lose focus and drift (and if I hate Hamden so much maybe I should stop hiding behind such a vainglorious vocabulary and anything-but-astute alliterations that don't impress anybody anyway), and that my self-exile at Hamden is mostly my own doing, despite the vodka. Which I at first found disappointing after all I had revealed, but then thought it might be worth further contemplation. Maybe I could, as time softened the reality of our relationship, perhaps remember our time together as something much more than just the anticlimactic odyssey of hopeful, heavenly, hormonal hijinks that so dominated our final days, confirming to me who I am.

I stayed put until it surprisingly occurred to me that when Chloe said that they plan your life maybe she wasn't talking about me at all (though all that other Hamden stuff was undoubtedly me), maybe she was talking about herself. Or both of us, as a shared thing to ease the embarrassment, maybe the way I did for her in our polluted-Chevy, cemetery retreat. Either way, whatever she was trying to say, it occurred to me that it really isn't about shared experiences to soften any blows, or even just avoiding reliving your parent's lives. It's deeper than that. What makes parent's lives something not to be relived? Whatever it was that made them who they are could very well make you who you are. Then it hit me.

Maybe that's what my father was trying to avoid when he let me take a childhood blast of vodka on the driveway all those years ago—he wanted me to taste what it would be like being him, and he knew I would hate it. And he wanted me to. All along I had been thinking it was just some stupid joke he was playing on me that was the best he could do.

Dammit, that was another one of those things he did for me, like letting me decide whether or not to play sports at Hamden. And I did decide that. Maybe I do have some impact on my own life after all; maybe there are some things I could decide for myself. Maybe my father was showing me just how to do that all along.

I wished Chloe would still be around so I could ask her what she thought about all that. Damn it! Since it was clear that there would be no answer without her, it seemed as good a time as any to start up the Chevy and head home, and not think too much more about Chloe Quinn for the rest of the day. And that's exactly what I did.

But not before I reached for my wallet and dug out that paper with the unfinished poem. I then grabbed the pencil that I had put in my glove compartment after our soggy, tree-lined kiss that seemed like forever ago because you never know when a girl like Chloe will once again inspire you, so you have to be prepared. And damn it if she didn't leave me with a final gift as I wrote down as quickly as I could, making a key change along the way:

> The rain upon the lips of leaves
> Does not cool the souls of trees.
> Burning limb to limb 'til now,
> 'Til nothing's left of crimson bough.
> Nothing's left, but long, black bones,
> To pierce a heart. And pierce my own.

After reading the poem over and over, I had decided to change my original line 'summer bough' to 'crimson bough.' Even though Chloe and I were most memorable during rainy, summer weather, well, the fact of the matter is that she and I were really more like autumn: a quick blast of beauty to be remembered forever, then gone for good.

I liked that line more and more and I committed it to paper so it would be fully documented for the ages. Even though I had changed it, Chloe showed me what it's like to be direct and honest, so I decided it best, as a tribute to her, to tell her honestly that we were crimson and she pierced my heart, no fancier words to get in the way.

I wanted her to know that, but I'd never tell her. Hell, I was pretty sure I'd never send her the poem. Besides, it has no title. While you can sum up a girl under a rainy tree in a poem, you can't reduce the whole thing any further to just a few words as a title. That just wouldn't be Chloe, or how I feel about her. But that's not so bad. I decided I could live with a title-less poem, and that's when I finally did start up the Chevy and head home. And I stopped thinking about Chloe Ellen Quinn, and crimson boughs, for the rest of the day. The whole damn day.

So how could I have been expected to jump right in with yet another, short-term, siren-like sensation, Nathalie, so soon after Chloe had left and while I was still processing her emotionally and poetically, and everything I did and did not become during our time together? I was not yet able to take the lessons learned from Chloe 101 and just haphazardly apply them to Nathalie, or anybody else, even if Nathalie was on her way out and I would never see her again either. That aspect did give me pause to reconsider for a moment but taking advantage of that opportunity would have required me to get even closer to her than I did to Chloe, enough to perhaps have reintroduced the need to grab handfuls of keepsake, tree-borne vegetation. But there was only so much foliage I was willing to carry around with me back then. Even now.

I think when someone leaves you forever, it's best you stop spinning endlessly for a while in order to make a full recovery, and so I did just that for the rest of the summer as best I could. Chloe was my first, so it was totally understandable that things might not have gone quite as planned, but that didn't mean that would always happen. And, sure, things didn't go much differently with Nathalie either, but that too can be explained away, like I had said, as happening too soon afterwards. Those kinds of things can happen to anyone, and they most certainly do. Who doesn't have a story of misplaced, mammary glands in their past, or open field, projectile vomiting blunders? And as incredulous as it may sound, once the tumultuous titillations of first-time, female familiarity faded (oops, some habits are just too hard to break), I was surprisingly looking forward to returning to the long-time comfort of my solitary confinement at Hamden to continue to work through who I was, as defined by that fizzling, sizzling summer heat wave, of sorts, that just passed.

I preferred to just sink back into myself with no new experiences to fire up any more anxiety. Especially since my encounter with Nathalie had curiously made me even more anxious than I would have expected, and revealed that my heart and nerves had also behaved the same way with Chloe (though certainly ratcheted up a notch), which didn't surprise me at the time, but maybe there was a connection? And speaking of connections, why did both of them choose me when other guys were present and I wasn't even trying, and I was ugly as hell, to boot?

The chukka boots. That had to be it. And their extra-tight-fitting nature, thanks to my flaccid little toe. I should have considered reigning in the extraordinary level of podiatry-related sex appeal that I apparently displayed quite freely, without any effort at all, mind you, and to which transitory, teenage temptresses seemingly are drawn. Maybe Chloe just meant even more to me than I thought, and I thought she meant a lot, that's probably why I was getting so anxious around another girl.

Yet the vodka king was at play too. I suppose I didn't really know that for sure, but what I did know was that I didn't like feeling nervous when big things came along, whatever those things might be. Ah, hell, enough. Full recovery, remember? Besides, gearing up for another fall at Hamden usually took me a whole damn summer anyway, and I still had plenty of time, so it always worked best for me if I was left to myself to do just that.

With junior year starting, I once again thought about the football season coming up and whether or not I was going to sense a fresh pressure to join the team. I wasn't going to back down from my refusal to play, nor was I going to entertain Chloe's diplomatic urging to consider bowling as an alternative, but I did have to process all my Chloe related, summertime, sexless exploits, so I had plenty to think about regardless. Not to mention the expected increase in critical, college related academics that I also had to consider, not so much to secure my future, but much more my present. After all, keeping Father-Vodka-Time off my back so I could ponder each passing Chloe-less month and evaluate the cumulative effect of unbridled humiliation on one's long-term identity was, without a doubt, my first priority of the new school year.

My only shred of identity at the time was, of course, my refusal to play on the Hamden football and baseball teams, and, I have to admit, I didn't entirely dislike the notoriety that followed me around, surely as defining as that of any other corduroy-jacketed-silk-stocking-upper-crust-prep-school ruffian so freely roaming the hallowed Hamden hallways in a most intimidating fashion. And I gotta also admit, a tiny part of me—make that a pretty damn big, whopping part of me—loved the fact that I had some ability that was coveted by Hamden to the point where they had actually believed their athletic standing in the prep school league might leapfrog to the upper echelons had I agreed to play alongside some of the other pretty talented kids that were finally showing up.

But I was not going to dole out any athletic contribution on my part whatsoever under any circumstances. Especially when my father had backed me up on that. I did dispense a little of it every once in a while, however, in pick-up games, just to stick it to them, which I always knew was a pretty chicken-shit thing to do, considering, as I mentioned before, that my classmates were really not all that bad.

Maybe I could have sucked it up a bit and played so that we all might at least have had a halfway decent chance to experience victory and ascension in the athletic world, to clearly accompany such ascension occurring, or soon to occur, in every other aspect of everyone's privileged life there. But, once again, ascension athletically, emotionally, academically, spiritually, philosophically, sexually, or any other 'ly' was not my path back then. And I was certainly nowhere near magnanimous enough to rise above all my overall, anxiety-drenched-stumblings, just to put those of privilege, or really anybody else for that matter, above my own inclination to bury myself as deep as possible so as to be totally unobservable by others—a ghost in plaid shirt and tie moving unseen among the masses, unknown but for the occasional, clumsy, off balance bump into misplaced objects and emotions alike, causing only a quick glance by other to see if something was there. Of course, nothing was—only me—so onward we all still go, the seen and unseen, until the next wisp of a collision.

But sometimes the plaid-shirt-and-tie sheet falls off. That can happen when a familiar, dentally challenged linebacker confronts you once more, not to welcome you into the circle yet again, more so to call you out on why you won't join the football team yet again at the start of this new year, and help the other guys try to win something they never won before (though the thought of a slew of banker's and lawyer's sons in desperate need of something other than money or connections does jar the senses and reaffirm that perhaps there really is a divine intellect up there).

But just when you thought you alone couldn't possibly be held responsible for any underperforming collection of private, prep-school, jock wannabes, you realize you were challenged in a quiet corner of an empty classroom and asked point blank to your face why you wouldn't join the team, accused in the same breath of thinking only of yourself. But then you realized you were left alone, as he walked away visibly confused and somewhat hurt that you wouldn't at least try to join, help, participate, et cetera. And all along the one thing that stuck in your mind, even more so than being confronted, was that he had the decency to approach you in private, and alone, not in a crowded hallway, or with a bunch of other Yale-bound thugs by his side to bully you into guilt or humiliation. No, he played it with a high level of dignity, and he left you standing there alone, as fully exposed as he must have sensed you were used to being, and while that at once made you feel as shitty as you should have felt, it also changed nothing. You wouldn't alter your position in any way.

I left the empty classroom and went on with my day, as did he, and all the others, all of us just trying to navigate through our still fragile and un-fully-formed lives despite the obvious optics of our community, and the heavy expectations placed upon all of us that, hoping to God, we wouldn't fail, or be discovered, or be humiliated, or forced to change our thinking that, regardless of cashmere sweaters and shiny cars, some people just aren't as bad as you desperately need them to be in order to justify your selected sense of self preservation. But how could he have known who I really was back then? I didn't. Still don't. I didn't play football or baseball because I could not adjust to full participation and acceptance into that life, that's all. No harm intended, dammit, even if I would have liked to believe that I was getting back at someone–anyone– that I could blame for the level of anxiety and confusion I lived every waking moment.

So, the one thing I could do, the one power I did have, apparently, was to withhold all of my perhaps overinflated sense of athletic ability? To lessen others around me? I just wanted to be left alone, that's all, to hide in the privacy of my own lack of understanding of why I was not like others, why I was overwhelmed by intimacy and preferred to withdraw, why I continually perseverated over every possible failure and experience that could define me, why I was so rigid about not accepting change, afraid to engage in what everyone my age did regardless of economic status: drink, smoke, date, buy condoms, don't use condoms but brag about using them, use them, hang out with the wrong people at the wrong time, make trouble. Graduate. Leave. That wasn't too much to ask, was it? Then I wouldn't have had to be in that position to stick it to my classmates, the headmaster, hell, the whole school for my shortcomings, because, of course, those who have nothing to do with your internal make-up and resultant behavior are most certainly the ones most responsible for it. No, I just wanted to hide.

Maybe I could've stuck it to my father for passing down the athletic ability that was destined to go to waste, but I couldn't even do that. Not too sure the basket of his DNA goodies left at my doorstep, courtesy of the United Skully Male Delivery Service, contained any athletic coordination whatsoever. And it certainly contained absolutely no dance–DNA, dammit. Dammit!

While I was pretty sure my father was really not the athlete I was, I most certainly was not at all the dancer he was. How could that have happened? What 'Good Ol' Dad' may have lacked out on the field he certainly more than made up for on the dance floor. He had moves! And stamina!

The few times I saw him and Mom cutting a little rug, they glided effortlessly, as if riding along some temporarily alcohol-suspended jet stream, two bodies melded into one, in what was most clearly a fantastic, publicly acceptable, physical expression of commitment to survive together, regardless of any struggle. Which made them, together while dancing, something that didn't seem to begin or end with either one of them, but was a quite surprising continuum of both of them together, further illustrating some kind of love deeply held at some truly rooted though not always visible level; a love surfacing only on stunning occasion, not unlike seventeen-year locusts (yes, twins, thanks to you, I know those specifically are really periodical cicadas); not to mention a love fighting for its life against the invasion of fermented spirits that somehow, and for reasons long unknown, burrowed their way into where they did not in any way belong. And all that was most evident at one of my cousin's weddings.

Seemed like every female in attendance had asked my father to dance after witnessing his prowess out there on the floor with mom, and he obliged them all, leaving no one hanging out to dry, until he had to excuse himself and retreat to the men's room to essentially hose himself down from sweaty exhaustion. But he twirled everyone who had asked him, and he gave each one a moment without compromise, and, dammit, I would trade every touchdown I ever scored or home run I ever hit to be my father's son when the music played. Instead, thanks (probably) to my mother, I have been presented with a ball and glove in place of Fred Astaire's most accomplished dance shoes. And (circling back to the dancing, crowned prince of vodka) a free pass as well to the free-fall thrills of lifelong guarded apprehension should you chose to punch that dance card, or have it punched for you.

My card was punched for Hamden, of course, so in junior year, while everyone pretty much blended into a neatly attired mass of prep school humanity, moving through the halls in a disorganized yet flowing herd from one class to the next: algebra to literature, advanced biology to ancient history, all of us awkward and gawky, the beneficiaries of increased higher learning and continued stubborn, progressive acne as we marched on toward graduation, something out of the ordinary happened. Adam Lastings emerged.

From years of short, neat, black hair, freckles, and a most unobtrusive personality, sitting in the back row of every class, not too far from me, Adam arrived as someone else, with longer, inky hair, a bit of a real swagger and attitude, same freckles, but now fully immersed in everything adolescence had to offer. Including a 1972, green, Ford Pinto.

Driving privileges arrived on campus, curiously enough, the same year the matured Adam arrived, screeching his car into a parking space, striding from car to school with sleeves rolled up, jacket slung over his shoulder, and constantly running a finger or two through his hair to keep it tucked behind his ears.

While everyone else mostly grew into the bodies they already inhabited while eschewing the customary, jungle-like locks and tresses of youthful, Vietnam-inspired, rebellion, preferring the more bank-friendly, short, snappy cuts instead, Adam and I, coincidentally, and independently, had grown our hair very long. Surprisingly, my father never once said anything to me about my hair, it being my one form of outwardly visible insubordination (presenting quite the conundrum of how to fit in and stand out at the same time while insisting, in my heart of hearts, that I not be noticed. My father, however, clearly noticed, how desperately I needed some breathing room).

Adam grew his, I'm sure to this day, to tuck his hair behind his ears such that his fully, freckled face might forever shine in the light of day, exhibiting a confidence not otherwise detectible in him in prior years. That '72 Pinto gave him a stature he wanted the whole world to see as well, racing through his whole demeanor, handling every tight curve of emerging self-determination, shining forever brightly in his eyes.

I, on the other hand, ensured my hair hung down as close to my face as possible so as not to reveal the vacuum of confidence in my eyes, hand covering my mouth while slumped in every classroom chair, arms pulled in tight, legs hidden under the desk as much as possible. I pretty much called upon any and every appendage to join forces once again and conceal any part of me that might otherwise invite friendship, or connection of any kind, the chukkas and their documented power over fleeting females notwithstanding. My withdrawal attempts didn't keep Adam away, though.

I started driving to school around the same time as Adam did, but our '64, family, Chevy tank (green like Adam's, curiously enough), mine once my parents got a new car to acknowledge our new eastern life, did not do for me what Adam's Pinto did for him, even considering earlier, Chloe-related escapades. No swagger associated with my newfound, school-bound mobility, just the empty, front, passenger seat where Chloe rode shotgun, once again in the most innovatively self-satisfying manner imaginable, and which I liked to keep free of any passengers in deference to the place of the first, official, East Coast sighting of the Ronkowski syndrome. So, no more buses for me, or sweet-smelling, grassy, long walks home from school anymore; I was my own master, all year long. Even during the winter months when the door locks of the Chevy would freeze shut and I had to roll down the windows and tie the doors together with my school necktie to keep them from opening in transit. Which was more than okay. I didn't need swagger, or any weather-resistant, National-Highway-Traffic-Safety-Administration approved door locks, I needed privacy, escape, and, yes, to continue to let Chloe go, if only little by little, and the Chevy during junior year provided all of that.

Despite my well-trained, classroom, body language, Adam and I were oddly and nevertheless being thrown together courtesy of circumstantial common ground: we both had green cars, we both had long hair, both were a bit rebellious—he outwardly, me inwardly—and we both sat as far back in the classrooms as possible, though that was more symbolic than effective when you only have eight to ten students per class and the back row is the second row.

Adam kept trying to connect, mistakenly thinking he had a kindred spirit of sorts in me, and I did begrudgingly start inching my way toward an acceptance of him (more so than a real friendship with him), but in a way that was more gravitational and unavoidable than sincere. I had been lucky to have side-stepped friendships up to that point at Hamden, and since Adam wasn't really connecting with the rest of the class in the same way he previously had been, though he was still staying largely on track for Ivy League life coming up just around the corner, maybe there was just some sort of mutually understood, underlying, sociopathic unity between us that was supposed to have mattered in ways neither one of us could have known at that time. So, one afternoon he wanted to test junior year driving privileges and skip study hall and go for a drive in his Pinto.

Still don't know why, but I agreed, from that purely gravitational standpoint only, of course, and probably in a most unguarded moment of once again trying on my nonexistent cool for a brief moment, even though that never worked with Chloe, though this was an entirely different circumstance. I realized I was risking my father's temper should he ever find out I chose a careless spree over extra study time, but grades were good, it was only study hall, it was a Friday, and off we went: jackets thrown in the back seat, front seat windows rolled down, elbows resting on the open-windowed door, arms bent up at an appropriately composed ninety degree angle, the geometry of which would have made Pounders proud, and hands resting where the top of the door met the roof, all of it to show the devil-may-care attitude that proclaimed we were totally comfortable and right where we belonged.

Adam took off out of the parking lot and down the street, heading for the winding back roads at as fast a rate as possible. The initial thrust plastered me against the front passenger seat as if being blasted off into space, and my attempted, cool demeanor was discarded recklessly out the window, replaced now with a totally new and unconvincing false poise, tipped off when my hand urgently relocated itself to the inside door handle in the form of a white-knuckled grip. (Considering the

G forces at work, I didn't think Chloe would have had quite the same front seat experience in Adam's Pinto as she enjoyed in the much more gravitational-force-per-unit-mass-friendly, however lumbering, Chevy.)

We raced through those back roads, Adam smiling and loving every minute, his hair tucked safely behind an ear, the only thing in that car even remotely resembling a safe place to stay put. He blasted the radio, the wind blew through the car, and we talked a bit in the new, free, harmonious movement of potential friends on their own, talking of nothing specific at first, he doing most of it, telling me about his girlfriend over at another school, the circumstances surprisingly not unlike Chloe's and mine, though his girlfriend was still around, and it occurred to me that not only was this indeed a new Adam from the one I barely knew before but had seen every day, this was a new opportunity as well. Most likely born from the underlying sense that while this was still junior year the end was approaching, nonetheless. I considered telling Adam about Chloe, but any force pulling us toward the center of a possible friendship did not yet outweigh the gravity of my experience with Chloe.

Adam had been at Hamden since kindergarten; me, of course, only since the eighth grade, though that was an eternity unto itself. Yet we were different now, both of us. Hell, maybe all of us. Everyone started bringing cars to school, and we all pretty much knew who everyone was by this time. Whether you were popular, quiet, an athlete, a scholar, a musician, an artist, a socialite, everyone was set and left to be whoever they were, and I was too. Adam did not try to deliberately draw me out in that Pinto front seat; he didn't ask me anything about why I was so quiet; he just talked, reveling in his newfound persona quite wholeheartedly, happy to unwittingly share it with some-one new, recognizing perhaps that he was changing into some-one else, shedding the young, good boy, student image, and enjoying a new path that appeared to be opening up to him, in a green Pinto, at break-neck speed, and with me in the front seat, no less. And with the end of Hamden days approaching, and the beginning of a new person required when entering whatever would come next, it appeared Adam was fully up to the challenge.

I finally relaxed a little in the Pinto, not feeling that I was changing nearly as much as Adam, but suddenly very content to see someone I barely knew changing joyfully, much more absorbed in his new growth, and I realized that everyone, in some way, was going through this--Adam just more visibly–but I wasn't, and wouldn't, deciding in my head once again that I would not by any means 'change', grow, move on, let go, embrace ... Hamden was moving on, and I would be left alone, safe in whom I was, and how I was trained to be. We returned to campus after about 45 minutes, stayed for a bit, then left for the day with no commitments to hang out, or do anything else in particular. Maybe I should've told him about Chloe. Maybe I still would.

A week later, on another Friday afternoon in September, I went out to the back field to play intramural touch football with a smattering of other kids from various grades, those who didn't want to play on, or couldn't make, the football, soccer or lacrosse teams in the Fall, and who usually found other less physical activities to do after classes ended, but were now required to obey the new Hamden rule that year of some athletic participation, no matter what your ability or level of interest. So, an after-school, pick-up, intramural program was set up, and all the Hamden-hanging-heads of forced participation lumbered out in shirt and tie to their required places. Surprisingly, with the football team winning their first two games of the season and looking pretty good, the Hamden powers-that-be left me alone to wander out onto the intramural field, throw the football around with whomever was willing to catch it, and kill the afternoon until we could leave.

Not much structure was in place when the whole thing started, which was pretty evident when the supervision of us lesser boys was bestowed upon eighty-one-year-old Mr. MacGregor, or Mr. Mac-G as he was known, with the rough, hewn face resembling sea-worn cliffs and an accent thick enough to warrant endless, poorly conceived imitations behind his back, and who surely played some meaningful role in the school, though nobody really knew what that was.

You usually saw him around the soccer team, monitoring a bag of balls and yelling at every kid who approached him, whether warranted or not, but that was about it.

When soccer season ended, he was even scarcer. But since he was clearly the most dispensable employee on the payroll all year round, he drew the short straw for inaugural intramurals, regardless of it coincidentally falling during soccer season, and off we all wandered, Mr. Mac-G already out in the field, barking instructions nobody regarded, and a baseball cap surprisingly tipped quite stylishly on his head to keep the sun out of that hopelessly craggy, spotty, and bumpy, bas-relief sculpture of a face. He called each of us by our last name cut there, with each annunciation making it quite clear that he was in no way even the least bit interested in pronouncing anyone's name correctly. It was hit or miss. When he got it right, you perked up for a moment, just in reverential acknowledgement of such a remote possibility; when he got it wrong, it cleared the conscience of any guilt of disrespect for ignoring him, since it was impossible to determine exactly whom he was addressing.

We got started amidst the dynamics of a wholly confusing communication as to just how this was supposed to work, so we all just milled about, tossing a ball that nobody really wanted to touch. And just when I was thinking that this might be the most completely stupid experience I was going to have at Hamden, causing me for the briefest moment to start to regret (if just a little, and for the very first time, I assure you) not joining the football team, though by now they had kids playing that, I have to admit, were really pretty damn good (and were perhaps rendering obsolete my notorious athletic stature at Hamden that so thoroughly defined me up to that point), a figure ran toward us from the building, getting closer, and tucking his hair behind his ears. When he got close enough, he ripped off his tie, threw his jacket on the ground, rolled up his sleeves, and, the moment I had the ball, he looked at me, ran out a little, clapped his hands once in that instantaneous communication that said "throw it!" without any words at all, and he kept running way beyond me, the other kids stopping to gawk, and Mr. Mac-G watching to see what was going to happen next.

What did happen next was exactly what I knew would, from that moment he threw his coat on the ground. I waited until he was as far out as some secret part of my brain could register was the limit of my throwing arm, and then I let loose a long, high, tight spiral, knifing right through the heart of that lingering, early September, sky. The ball arced up, floated weightlessly, then eased down over his left shoulder, and Adam hauled it in without breaking stride. All the other kids watched dumbfounded as he circled back toward us. Then he waved me out, and he returned the favor, and he and I threw that ball around wordlessly, as far as we could, challenging our arms with each throw. Mr. Mac-G recognized that this was not going to stop, so he dragged the bag of remaining footballs over and spilled them on the late summer grass for the others to do with them whatever they could while Adam and I owned the one field that most likely mattered most that afternoon. And well beyond.

Since Adam had been at Hamden ever since he was a small kid, Mr. Mac-G seemed to know his last name, but, not too surprisingly, he had to keep asking me mine. He finally gave up on mine, and when he wanted to call us both, or either one of us separately, since we were always together out there anyway, he just yelled, "Lasky!"

Apparently, he wasn't emotionally ready yet, or willing, to put in the extra effort respectfully required to produce either Lastings or Skully distinctly, delivering instead a sort of lazily conjoined, auditory hallucination (though admittedly passable), which neither Adam nor I wanted to acknowledge we heard at first. But we quickly picked up on Mr. Mac-G's preference for indifference toward butchered annunciation when summoning anyone sixty plus years his junior, so "Lasky!" became as real and familiar as our own individual last names, however deeply lost to the spotty, cerebral callings of the persistently scowling octogenarian.

I was stunned to see Adam come out to the field that day. Apparently, his new persona included ditching the football team he, too, played on in eighth grade, and for a few years more after that. He was indeed now a new person and trying on his new life, in all aspects. I wondered if anyone else from our class might join the intramural club, but nobody else did, and the football team was, without a doubt, beginning to take on a new winning identity all its own, without Adam, who didn't seem to care in the least, and certainly without me. True, Adam and I had a field of our own now, despite using it for different reasons (one for busting out into the sunlight of a newfound freedom; one for running from the light of day), but I had never expected the football team might actually move on without me.

As Adam and I threw around the football that day, I was surprised at how good it felt to let loose and fully utilize what athletic ability I had, however solitary the experience.

I broke a mild sweat in the late day, warm sunlight, my muscles relaxing more and more, feeling fluid and loose, and I reveled in the afternoon as much as one could in a plaid, flannel shirt and tie, jacket on the ground nearby. Had my father not freed me from the pressure to join the team, I might not have had such momentary joy. Surely it didn't exist in the same manner at all in pads and drills, regardless of how well the team was now doing without me, but there in the wide expanse of the intramural field, under the last teasing warmth of the season, far enough down field to be removed from all that was Hamden for just an instant, including the newfound, winning ways of the football team, the moment was illuminating and overwhelming. I thought again of my father. I really wanted my athletic ability to have come from him. In the sun-washed magnificence of the field, I instantly wanted that bond of playing ball, any kind of ball: football, baseball, basketball, anything he and I could do, but that was surely not going to be the case.

The few times we had shot baskets together in the driveway behind our house he had mostly avoided shooting. I didn't realize it then. He rebounded my shots and fed them back to me, giving me all the chances. After I sat down in the cool grass to catch my breath on one occasion, though, he grabbed the ball, went to what would have been the foul line, and he shot a few. My father was awkward. He shot straight out from the chest, moving no other part of his body while leaning heavily into his shot such that, upon release, he had to lunge, then step forward desperately with a long stride, to avoid falling flat on his face (not unlike my closing dance moves in Chloe's pest friendly basement), the ball then bouncing off the backboard every time, without scoring a bucket at all. My father did not have the ability. Or so I thought, before our Hamden, multi-continental, point guard, by pure coincidence, happened to be showing off his untouchable knowledge of basketball during one afternoon gym class, when coach was late, by imitating the passing and shooting styles utilized across the decades, focusing on what, to him, were the most comically employed ones of all: the 1930s lunging chest pass and the alley-oop type shot, from the ground up, known most affectionately as the "granny shot." I had watched him in stunned silence as he unknowingly imitated my father's shots. And then it occurred to me that maybe my father knew all along that the style he was used to using, as a child, would no longer inspire fear in any opponents whatsoever. He might have very well missed on purpose (or at the least was understandably a bit rusty) so that my shots going in would have effectively acknowledged a passing of the athletic torch, of sorts.

Despite basketball being the only sport I was, at least, mildly involved in with my father, he had a non-basketball childhood nickname: Galloping Ghost, like Red Grange, which had always confused me, but maybe made more sense than I knew. He told me the neighborhood kids gave that to him when he was about nine years old, and he always said it with such pride, it being an obvious title of supreme football talent, and then just athletic ability in general. But he seemed to struggle athletically, as I had witnessed over and over again, at least seemingly so in basketball, and I had wondered if he was given that name as a joke that he himself did not realize, carrying along with it a self-pride that was unfounded.

I didn't like thinking that about my father because I wanted him in his most innocent and free years to have been gifted, and aware of it, and happy. I wanted him to have pronounced that nickname with a deeply self-satisfying pride based on externally acknowledged ability. Maybe that might have helped avoid the vodka pitfalls later on, who knows? I wanted to think that, and I didn't like the creeping thought of any of his childhood friends snickering behind his back at something he wasn't aware of, making a fool of the child who would be my troubled father, laughing the way the other kids on the Hamden intramurals field did behind Mr. Mac-G's back, in his case making fun of his accent and surely his age.

Maybe my father was better at football than basketball, though; maybe that's why he was crowned with a football nickname. We never did play that together, but then again full-contact, tackle football between father and son as an after-dinner frolic isn't nearly as prevalent as one might think. But maybe he was just an athletic product of his time, which we all ultimately are (and all of which ultimately fades), no better or worse than me. And, dammit, if it wasn't a Hamden classmate, of all people, who unwittingly introduced me to the notion that perhaps my father was more than I realized, not unlike how Chloe did, in her own way, though his was more accidental while hers was a direct hit. I didn't, and still don't, really know about that, but either way, when you mix in the things a father perhaps does knowingly for his son with the things a father does unknowingly to his son, well, how are you going to decide how you're supposed to feel about it all? I doubted there were any annoyingly all-knowing athletes in Hamden who could've given me the answer to that. Though Chloe probably could have.

When intramural time was up, Mr. Mac-G started gathering the balls and the other kids started heading home.

Adam and I continued to throw the ball around after everyone had gone, and Mr. Mac-G stood out there and let us throw for as long as we wanted. When finally we had to head in, Mr. Mac-G yelled his signature, "Lasky!" and we both came trotting in. We put our ball in the bag with the others. Adam took the bag from Mr. Mac-G and said, "I got it," and carried the bag for him back to the school.

I grabbed our jackets and ties off the ground, a few steps behind Adam and Mr. Mac-G. The two bantered back and forth; I could tell Mr. Mac-G liked Adam. I kept to myself but was damn glad all the other kids were gone. I didn't want to hear anybody laughing at Mr. Mac-G. When we got back to the school, Adam took his jacket and tie from me.

"See you Monday," he said.

"You mean, Tuesday." I cleared my throat.

"Oh, right, three-day weekend, excellent! See you Sweet Potato Tuesday! Don't forget to study." He laughed, then he turned around, and while walking backwards toward his car, he added, "Hey, you should party with us sometime."

He didn't wait for my answer and took off in his Pinto. I wasn't going to answer anyway, and I drove off in the Chevy. I thought I might pass by the football practice field on my way home, for no particular reason, but then I thought better of it. I rolled down the front windows to get a cross breeze going, and I headed home. It was so damned warm outside.

All the way home, I kept thinking about Adam's invitation to party and who this "us" really was. Was he not as self-isolating as I perhaps thought he was becoming in his new persona, not my sociopathic comrade to be? Maybe there were some kids from Hamden that he still hung around with after school; maybe his "us" were some friends he had outside of Hamden with his girlfriend, much like the neighborhood and public-school friends I had. Was that something additional we had in common, our social construct? Even if that were so, I was not going to hang with Adam outside of school. I didn't really hang out with him much in school, even though I have to admit that he was okay, but I was not going to allow all the work I had done over the years to successfully insulate my-self from Hamden crumble to pieces over one potential, new-found, kindred spirit of sorts. No, I'd rather hold out and start anew somewhere in college, once and for all safely leaving all of Hamden behind, letting it fade away to its logical vanishing point, whenever that would be, never bringing anyone from that school along with me into my later life. Because Hamden was something I just had to get through, that's all.

But I kept wondering just who else Adam hung out with, maybe some preppy kids I shared classes with? Maybe the linebacker? What about the twins?

Hopefully not Plugger. What if it were the Italian kids I knew from elementary school who were here now? Could that work? I didn't know. Besides, I had successfully compartmentalized all the kids I grew up with, and I had a place for each of them: the Illinois kids, my public-school friends (like I said before), my neighborhood friends, the Hamden kids. They all had a unique place in my experiences, and they did not overlap or intersect in any way, shape, or form. My life seemed to have developed that way, and I preferred to keep my social interactions completely independent of each other; a mingling of any two or more groups would have disrupted the comfort level I demanded in order to keep my anxiety level at a controllable pace. That whole approach had threatened to come a bit unglued, admittedly, when I first got to Hamden and noticed a few kids there from my public-school life, but I quickly adjusted by not interacting with them very much at all, keeping them in a special sub-compartment as a potential one-time only exception, which I never did anything about, however.

And just how did Adam's "us" party anyway? If it was Hamden kids, did they drink and smoke and boast about who had the biggest bank account? Did they date according to the generally accepted principles of privileged, teenage, automotive hierarchy—certain German or Italian cars being the top rung? Based on Adam's Pinto, I'm guessing there were few if any Hamden kids in his collective, partying "us" after all, but there was no doubt that smoking and drinking were involved and, not unlike the vodka-inspired terror of accidental, teen-aged fatherhood that so permanently hung over my unsettled head, underage, alcoholic leanings of any sort, no matter how ultimately uneventful, would have still given early, fatherhood fear a run for its money in our house. I'm guessing a teenage son coming through the doors totally plastered, hammered, or tanked at the same moment a father swirls then swallows his last nightcap would have been a tad too close to home to let slide for the father, and certainly an overwhelming risk for the son. Not to mention a catastrophe for the mother.

The one time I did come home under the influence (my first, full encounter with the distilled, spiritual world, shared most amiably with a few of the neighborhood kids in one of their less rodent-free, however finished, basements while their parents were out) my mother's antennae went straight up. The tension in the house was quite palpable when later that same night that my father was due home from a business trip she suspected misdoings, hearing me clunking around the bathroom, laughing far more than I ever do, seeing the bathroom light shining under the door for a lot longer than would be explainable under even the most understandably trying, gastronomical conditions. I did try and pull myself together and put myself in her place, and the decision she was faced with when she knocked on the bathroom door, but that was a bit of a challenge, considering nature's most untimely, highly prolonged, yet dismally fruitless calling, the timing of which I found hopelessly hilarious.

Sitting stone drunk, though quite contentedly, on the throne, pants harmlessly gathered at my ankles, I swung open the door and most unabashedly asked her, with as straight a face as possible, "Whaddya want?" The visual of me sitting there, most dutifully, immediately confirmed her suspicion, I'm quite sure, and clearly put her in a tough spot while not endearing me to her in any way whatsoever, despite my most supportive, however queasily inviting, accessibility. It did, however, most assuredly, add to her anxiety level because, despite my condition, I could surprisingly still see that she was terrified of what might happen should my father encounter this scene upon arrival home from a trying and tiring week-long business trip, it being her responsibility, now, to extricate me freely and expeditiously from the comfort and warmth of a most accommodating, luxury, slow-close, toilet seat ring, yet another perk from our privileged eastern life.

And she was determined to do so, even if that meant I'd lose some skin off my ass during the prying process, so fixed, she was, on quickly reintroducing me to the spinning room that had so nicely settled down upon my seating choice, but which could very well return at a moment's notice upon my standing up—once again a most unfortunate posture at a most inopportune time.

And who knew bathrooms and Junior High moonlit fields were equally troublesome locales in which to remain upright under what would otherwise be, for most anyone in either situation, quite the triumphant circumstance, though not for me. Pressed into post-potty, perpendicular posture, prematurely, I could hear that familiar terror in my mother's voice, knowing both of us would be the recipients of my father's displeasure from seeing his son in such a personally recognizable state of inebriation that was now no laughing matter. I tried to sober up, as best I could. No matter what your state of mind, if you know you're in trouble, that's one thing, but when your mother will take an equal, though certainly undeserved, share of the oncoming wrath that unquestionably belongs to you, heightened by a father's unexpected look-in-the-mirror, of sorts, upon first glimpse of his sufficiently stewed son, well, that's just too much guilt to contain. This was not a mother on a weepy stairwell being processed by a seven-year-old mind; this was not a critical decision on a front lawn about whether to team up and leave the vodka king behind, a clearly fatal move that wasn't even under serious consideration; this was a case of incurring yet another round of unpredictable terror while remaining captive, and fully subject to its wrath.

Even in my state, I could see that, suddenly, this was it. This was it! (what, again?) The one thing I could do at last. Save her! Finally! And me, too, perhaps, from this specific, brewing storm cloud, by completely regaining myself. After all she wasn't in the least interested in punishing me, or saving herself, she was interested in saving me! But I had to do the saving; it was up to me. I tried my best to exit the bathroom expeditiously, but I miscalculated the door opening a tad, despite its adherence to generally accepted, building code standards–standards being critical for bathrooms and rubbers alike, and I walked directly into the left-hand doorjamb, leading with my forehead, and a strong sense of determination, and sending upon impact quite the loud, dead thud into the tense night.

Most surprisingly, and much to her credit upon my teetering back in confusion as to who would stick a doorjamb in such a ridiculous spot so as to purposely impede sprightly exiting, however tipsy, foot traffic, my mother chose determination of her own versus motherly compassion. "Ogden, stop fooling around!" she barked, her outburst confirming her resolve while conjuring up an image of the two of us outside the Lincoln bedroom once more.

And, apparently, though quite mystifyingly, accelerating tension coupled with youthful, bodily misfires is the trick that remarkably reveals an underlying, and quite surprising, sense of authority in my most puzzling, helpless, brave, lonely, and heroic mother. To which I, just like my pre-pubescent, ever nervous, roiling, White House stomach, would unquestionably succumb. Because you can't do anything that would drag a most complicated, strong, yet admiringly vulnerable, person like her into all your mistakes. Anything. She will allow the dragging, and she will suffer for it, in her way, trying to save you, and you just don't know how much suffering a mother

can take, and does take, and you surely don't want to be responsible for any of it. Not only will it make you feel like shit
when you realize what you've done to her, but it's too damned
overwhelming when you see her get up the next morning and
do the things for you that she always does, no matter what,
and always will do without ever really blaming you for causing
her pain.

Because she knows the real source.

Which can quite convincingly make you realize that maybe
your favorite memory of your mother shouldn't be of her
standing at the top of the stairs, trying to be what you define
as an adult in your seven year-old eyes, though you can't blame
a seven year-old for that, or her effort to save you from your
own youthful, liquid, exploratory activities that park you in a
bathroom; no, it should be more of those things she does every
day, without you even considering what it takes to do them.
And just when you thought, however embarrassingly smugly,
that you had it all figured out about what it takes to be an
adult, the definition was right under your nose all the time, in
the most obvious way. Any mother hurting at the top of the
stairs was most likely always an adult, even if not in the way
you thought you needed at that point in your life.

And while there are a lot of defining moments that most
encounter in adolescence, and remember somewhat fondly for
the way they grew from that point forward, once they were
a safe enough distance from the initial impact, realizing that
persuasive, bonding, boozy, bathroom behavior was all it took
to forge you and your mother into allies at last, if only for
that one night, fighting together for survival instead of fleeing
together from a front lawn against a common enemy who,
by the way, had inappropriate, unwarranted, and undeserved
roughness forced upon him, without his consent, to unfairly
make him who he is, is a different kind of teenage experience
altogether. The result of which, despite the initial, fortified

feeling of having a newfound partner in crime by your side, is sadly one that you may never grow up from, grow away from, or gain any higher knowledge from whatsoever, because all it means is that there are three very lonely people living in the same house. And there's no vanishing point for that. But you knew that. And, trying as the parental, adult two of the three might to recognize it and change it all under the guise of a new eastern life, some things just happen too late in life, no matter how early in your life they happen.

So, as a result, I was not going to be any more friendly with Adam Lastings than the school day demanded. Like I said, I pretty much had all my other grouped friendships under control, and Adam was new to the whole mix, so I couldn't bring any more tension into the house by joining a new friendship group that most certainly would have involved paying some sort of alcoholic dues up front, dues that might've planted me firmly, and quite riskily, though certainly most enjoyably, however urgently, once again upon a most comfortable, albeit potentially physically and emotionally explosive, eastern variety toilet seat. I could not do that to my mother. Again. Once was fine, and probably important to us both, but to press her into allied service on a continual basis, especially involving indoor plumbing, would be too much for her to endure, and far too cruel an undertaking just to open my social circle a little, if that was even possible.

I had to let my newfound camaraderie with my mother go, I had to, no matter which one of us ultimately saved the other, if either of us did that at all, so she could find her own place of comfort. I could not endanger her any more deeply than I just did (after all, the usual motherhood dangers run pretty damn deep all by themselves). Which meant I had to let Adam go, too, before he became another Kenny and I perhaps would open up about Chloe, which, I admit, was a bit of a relief, and a lot easier than trying to be someone I really wasn't. And so, I did let the friendship go, though he never knew it. And I would never get it back. Even when you think you're doing the right thing because it's the only thing you can do, and even when it becomes much clearer later on why a Friday afternoon on a lonely intramural field was to be so memorable, you still can't get some things back. Shit.

That weekend right after Adam and I had thrown around the football was still pretty unseasonably warm, but on Tuesday when I got into the Chevy to head to Hamden Hell there was a slight chill in the air, a comfortable coolness that pretty much told you the last four days were but a taste of what once was but was not to be again. I started up the car and headed out.

Pretty quiet weekend, I kept thinking in the soft early morning, got caught up on my homework, started reading the collection of poetry assigned for an upcoming Lit class, and studied for the possible quiz in algebra based on Pounders' latest, lame, lunchtime inspired proclamation. But as I approached Hamden, my heart began to sink a little, as usual. I had Pounders first thing, 8:30am, and I didn't want to be late, especially on the day of a potential quiz, which was hard enough to focus on given the aforementioned breathability of the classroom, but also because he likes to call you out by thanking you for deciding to join the class. When I pulled into the parking lot, I think I must have glanced around subconsciously for Adam's Pinto because something felt a little odd. I didn't see his car, but I figured he was late and racing to school to make up for lost time. I thought about last Friday and throwing the football around, and was even reconsidering telling him about Chloe, but then I abruptly stopped. Hurry up, can't be late! I quickened my step through the parking lot and across the street to school, not wanting to fully sprint to attract any attention, but I should have run because I didn't see anyone outside, so I was definitely late. Dammit, not today.

I went up the stairs into the school, took a deep breath, opened Pounders' door, and snuck in, hoping to find a back seat, but they were all taken. The class was quiet, the air thankfully free of any Pounderly, post-consumption contaminants whatsoever. Mr. Pounders sat at his desk and surprisingly didn't say anything. He wore a gray suit with no lab coat and his hair was noticeably, nicely combed. He looked suspiciously presentable and quite nice, as if he had been pre-informed of something dire and had dressed accordingly, as one does at the beginning of sorrow.

I found my seat and sat down in the heavy silence. I did not at all like what I was seeing: no greeting, no real noise, nobody sent up to the blackboard. A few kids shifted in their seats. Mr. Pounders sat still and finally looked up at the class. Then he said without any preface, but with a genuine sincerity that frightened me and forever connected me to him in a way in which he would never know, "I'm so distraught over the Lastings boy."

That was all I heard, I didn't know who filled in the details, and when, but the class never fully materialized, and Sweet Potato Tuesday's test was cancelled. Quite to Pounders' credit, he never used that phrase again in deference to its association with a day we all were collectively, though unintentionally but upon hearing the news of Adam's death necessarily, and perhaps divinely, diminished.

We were dismissed early from class and went to study hall. By then we all knew that Adam had gone out Saturday night with a buddy, driving his Pinto. Nobody knew for sure, but word was that he went to the bar in that popular restaurant that everyone knew served minors, and he drank and drove home, racing down Sawyer Lane at seventy miles-per-hour, which is the most narrow, windy road in the back country, with a speed limit of no more than 20 miles-per-hour. Adam lost control of the car; it flipped over, throwing both riders out of the car, the passenger landing largely unhurt up against a nearby tree, but the Pinto landed on Adam, killing him instantly, killing Adam Lastings with the great football hands, at seventeen years young, on a clear, calm, last, warm September Saturday evening, while I was at home. Doing nothing. On an otherwise cruelly relaxing three-day weekend.

The school day continued in disarray. Classes tried to be held in the usual fashion, but the teachers, much to their credit, left the time open for anyone who wanted to talk about what had happened. Homework was delayed, tests were postponed, and we spent a lot of time in study hall, just reading or doing homework, until the headmaster came in and told us there would be a memorial service later in the week that we would all attend. We were to show up at school at the usual time; we would be bussed over to the First Congregational Church for the service, bussed back, and then we could leave for the day, or remain in school, in study hall, if we preferred.

I spoke to no one about the details, or how I felt, I just continued to try and process what had happened, how Adam could throw a football around with me one Friday afternoon, being fully alive, his hair flying madly in the breeze and disobeying his futile attempts to tame it and keep it behind his ears while he ran full speed out into an empty field with no one around, waiting for my pass, waiting, running, beaming … waiting … living fully for his last day, not knowing he was leaving, no idea he would be gone in just another day. It was warm, he was running, he was alone, far out in an empty field, in late sunlight, and I saw him, way out there, in such bright light: free, happy, emerging, blooming, leaving, falling away, absorbed in light. "Throw it!" he seemed to yell with no words at all, and I did, the football arcing up into Adam's last day; it left my hand, it left me, it sailed, it arced, it found him, and he caught it and kept running with it until he returned to us; no, he never returned, he left, he went away, the rest of us stayed, we were here, I was here, left to explore the incomplete, the dangerous, the glorious and, yes, the shattering, all on my own. Still on my own. He was seventeen, and he went away. I was the last one at school to see him and talk to him late that Friday afternoon. "See you Sweet Potato Tuesday." He had laughed. He had lied.

I never knew what to do about the experience. I went to school the rest of the week; everyone did. It was solemn. We went to Adam's service, piled out of quiet, yellow buses, and filled in a few pews reserved for us. Adam's family sat in the front row. His parents were stoic, until our prized baritone went up to the altar, his ever-present smile replaced with a transfixed focus and total absorption of the enormity of the moment, and he sang Schubert's "Ave Maria" in stunning brilliance, the elegiac quality of the melody superbly delivered.

Everyone was immediately transformed by some level of grace that the song, delivered uniquely in the baritone's most comfortable register, conveyed in an instant, though we felt as if we had all along been under its healing canopy without discernable beginning or end. His voice soared, as if carrying Adam's soul with it because there was clearly no other metaphysical explanation for the immediate uplift in mind, body, and the collective spirit of the gathering.

Nothing could have made Adam more singularly perfect in that moment, and the rest of us hushed in humility at the presence of some form of greater transcendence. I don't know that anyone present had ever witnessed such an overwhelming gift as the one our baritone gave Adam's family.

Adam's sister wept; his mother wept; his father briefly collapsed in grief, both sister and mother immediately securing him upright in his seat. I thought instantly of my father in the same situation, and it completely unnerved me to imagine such a scene and the love that must burn so deeply despite arguments, fights, disagreements, anything that would play counterpoint to a parent's vision of what is best for their child, regardless of the child's desires, such that a physical and emctional collapse would be the last exit from grief a human heart could employ, however unsuccessfully, in its personal riot against such betrayal. I felt out of place, like I was intruding upon a grand intimacy never intended for a family, but called into place, nonetheless. I decided I would go home after the service, needing to be away from Hamden and the lingering power of Adam's departure and its effect on everyone I was with that day.

Just looking at my classmates on the bus ride back, most of whom I still knew nothing about, and was sure I would never even remember after graduation, made me realize that, regardless, we would all be forever connected now. Through the absence of Adam Lastings.

Once the bus arrived at Hamden, our class scattered: some stayed, some left. I gathered my books from my locker and started to head out. The twin from my Lit class had his locker close to mine and was there at the same time I was.

He looked over at me and said that he had seen Adam and me on the field from the study hall window on that Friday that seemed forever ago. "You guys were good," he had said. He then closed his locker and left. While it was pretty clear he was trying his best to say something of comfort and connection, I was surprised at how difficult that seemed to be for him, as if he had expected he could have done better and should have. But I was even more surprised that someone saw us out in the field in a moment that I had assumed was invisible to others and had belonged to just Adam and me (under the approving eye of Mr. Mac-G only) in a sort of temporary camaraderie that seemed to have a feel of purpose to it, even while it was happening, though who knew what that was at the time, or even now. And I didn't like that we had been seen by someone else thereby keeping Adam and I externally connected forever.

And I couldn't help it at all, but I just didn't want to have any connection to Hamden, especially one of poignancy that others might remember, maybe forever. But, dammit, if anyone had to see us with the football that day, at least it was someone I had an odd feeling I could trust would do nothing more with the experience, or eventual memory, than possess it in the respectful silence in which it was intended to occur, to preserve my desired anonymity and minimal connection to others while I processed what had just happened.

I really didn't know what to do with the twin's condolence; it was both unwelcome and acceptable. I hated things that were polar opposites that you were stuck with and couldn't draw any satisfying or enlightening conclusions from. Still do. I decided to think quite heavily about it some more while I drove home, much in the way I used to ponder grass, and other important topics, while walking home from Hamden. I went out of my way to drive the same road that Adam and I had driven together that one day in his Pinto, to give me more time to think before I got home and, quite honestly, to deeply imbed in me so as to never forget the overwhelming realization that had I agreed to be friends with Adam, and had I partied with him or his group, I might have, well, you know ... there was a passenger in that car, and, yes, he was only hurt, but who knows if that would have been my outcome? Maybe it was a good thing we never became friends; maybe I've been disconnecting myself from Hamden for a good reason, after all. Yet, despite my best efforts, everything still happened. Dammit, if only Chloe were here, I wouldn't have to deal with this alone.

Truthfully, though, I probably wouldn't have told her a damn thing.

Classes eventually returned to normal, slowly, but they did return. Voices filled the hallways, steps were hurried, not slowly dragged, at some point some level of silliness and laughter re-emerged, and the Hamden that gave the Lastings a full level of sincere respect said its goodbye and returned to the living. Homework that was reassigned was now being handed in, tests that had been postponed were now being administered, and a plaque was respectfully installed in the auditorium that read "Adam Lastings, In Loving Memory." Everything got back to normal in what seemed like both a quick turnaround and an eternity, leaving not nearly enough time to process the enormity of the event properly, but too much time to dwell upon it aimlessly.

I don't think I went back to intramurals that year. I didn't want to be out there in that empty field, holding a football with no one to throw it to. I didn't recall seeing Mr. Mac-G out there in later weeks either, though some kids were out tossing balls around. I stayed in study hall the rest of the time, and Hamden didn't say a word, and the football team kept winning, still undefeated, and I found myself drifting further and further away from any athletic based identity, or any connection to the school, whatsoever.

It appeared, though, that normalcy was indeed fully reinstated and that despite my continued withdrawal that very same normalcy might perhaps, however illogically, absorb me and protect me in its cushion against this and any other severe blows that might come out of nowhere. That seemed to be the case at first, while I was in study hall Friday of that horrible week (everything seemed to happen on Fridays at Hamden), going over the assigned poems for the first time since the prior week in order to prepare for a final review coming up in Lit class the next period before we would move on from poetry. There were a few obscure and lesser-known poems to study, and I came across a poem titled "Dust" by Rupert Brooke. I vaguely remembered glancing over it more than a week ago, but I needed to read it again. And I did. I read it. And my heart began to mysteriously race. And I felt a little sweaty.

I read the opening line about some white flame being gone, and I squirmed a little in my seat. Then there was a line about losing the world's delight. And then I read the line "When your swift hair is quiet in death" and my heart pounded, and my breath shortened. This was far worse than any nervousness I had experienced with Chloe or Nathalie, or even in Adam's memorial service. So much panic filled my head and heart upon reading that one line, especially, and though I had no idea what was going on I was certain the whole study hall was staring at me. Thousands of eyes.

I felt this tremendous rush of sorrow, or emotion, or anxiety—I didn't know which one—and my heart hammered away mercilessly. Everything that had happened over the last weeks, maybe even longer, was rushing right back up again in that singular moment, and I had no idea why.

Things had been settling down; I seemed to handle Adam's death okay, I thought; the worst was certainly over; what was happening? I couldn't breathe. I couldn't stop my heart, and I began to get nauseous. And scared. I needed to get out of there. Just like in the field with Chloe! But worse. What's happening? I pushed out from the desk and grabbed my books, and I hurried out of the room, not knowing where to go. I just needed to get away from anyone—everyone—watching me, so I stepped outside into the fresh autumn air, and I tried to breathe. I had to be alone—alone was the only place I knew.

Surprisingly, no one stopped me, and no one was outside. I paced the schoolyard between the main building with the study hall and most of the classrooms and the old garden basement building where my Lit class was going to be. I took deep breaths, but my heart still beat quite noticeably.

Nothing was really working; the return to normalcy at Hamden was apparently no return at all for me. "With all thy getting, get understanding ..." How? When? I was left alone with Adam's death, and it seemed to be going okay for a bit, but everything had happened so fast that I apparently never had time to process his passing, even though I thought I did, and no level of "normalcy," no matter how quickly re-established, was able to take that away.

Why did I have to be so connected to Adam in a field and with a football that it would lead to this? God, please get me through this. I wanted desperately to leave; I wanted to go home, but I couldn't go to the office and ask to be excused, they'd see me like this. I didn't want anyone to know. I couldn't be seen. Like with Chloe in that field, I did not want anyone seeing my face at its most vulnerable. Please get me through the next class, last of the day, of the week.

Please.

I tried to calm myself as best I could, and I actually began to tremble a bit less. Maybe I can do this, I thought. I stayed outside until the bell rang, and teachers and students once again filled the halls and yard, running to their next class, and I headed toward mine. But what if we talk about this poem? I can't. I cannot. I kept telling myself I wasn't going to make it after all as I approached the stairs to the oddly placed Lit class in the garden basement building. I steadied myself as best I could as I started to walk down the stairs, and then the door opened and up and out and into the golden autumn sunlight she rose.

No one else was on the stairs, and she and I passed dangerously close, and she was the girlfriend of the richest kid in our class, and everyone knew it, and the same sun that illuminated Adam just weeks ago caught the fine hair on her thigh. Our shoes almost touched, and she looked at me, and she said, "Excuse me," in that most sincere voice, while carrying Dante, and my heart's deliverance was successfully accomplished, with great mercy, and she smiled ever so lightly, I'm sure, and she was totally unobtainable and oh, so close, and we would never meet again, this closely or otherwise, oddly enough, in such a small community, but that moment was suddenly, and most blessedly, safe, and deep, and stirring, and safe, and, yes, oh yes! I needed to be safe; oh, how I needed to be safe! I needed to desire something so unobtainable so as to never risk experiencing any intimacy, or new connection, in a field, or anywhere else, that would send me running out of a study hall again.

Adam's death was so overpowering, acting like a Trojan horse of sorts, all my recent losses packed inside, waiting to pounce. And pounce they most assuredly did, in the heavy quiet of a cavernous, empty study space that was supposed to be a safe place to absorb what you learned, at your own pace, but was anything but that during that afternoon. And I needed to be forever safe from anything that might happen to me because I can't handle things that do happen to me.

And up and out she rose, and down I went into Lit class, my directionless heart and embarrassingly, though harmlessly, excitable pants leaping from despair to new, unexpected life in what must have been the exact same measure of time that Adam went from life to death, that eternal fleeting transference his heart surely encountered upon complete and irreversible transformation into magnificence, becoming one with his spirit in perhaps the most overwhelming coalescence imaginable, most surely captured, or accompanied, or underscored, by the baritone's uniting hymn, delivered in perhaps equal splendor. For Adam. For me? "She," the Orpheus stairwell girl, was the opposite of Chloe, and how I was revealed to be disappointingly who I am; "she" was the opposite of Adam, and how I without permission was placed in an overwhelming position, far greater than myself, that I was most likely not equipped to handle; and, yes, "she" was eternal innocence. and everything and anything that could never happen, replacing everything I knew I must steer clear of. And never, no, never, I was most profoundly convinced, absolutely never lose who you are—not now, not ever—don't risk becoming someone other than the one you know so well. And the Orpheus stairwell girl saved me, unbeknownst to her, by presenting herself as something I could never have. Ever. And it felt so free and instantaneously liberating to desire something that would require nothing whatsoever from the heart. Nothing at all. And that's what I wanted most.

I'm not at all sure how that Lit class finally ended. My stomach churned and I fought hard to distract myself, when required, focusing on the stairwell encounter and it perhaps being maybe nothing more than just some sort of sign I desperately needed to get through class. Maybe I had been making way too much of it. Getting through class was all I wanted, and I immediately liked the idea of reducing something I thought was so big to something more urgently useful, especially while being in public with the potential to reveal inner angst. I could work with that; I was in need of something easy and that would do it. Sometimes, reducing something is the best thing you can do for yourself when around others; you can always revert to the original intent when you're safely and uncontrollably alone again, which I most certainly did, and to this day have grown quite comfortable with.

But just as I was getting settled with this notion, the class, much to my nervous anticipation, then indeed started talking a little about the Brooke poem. And just when I felt my nausea beginning to resurface as the discussion began, immediately negating the Ogden Skully Reduction Theory, the twin who had been outside my locker when we had returned from Adam's service earlier in the week brought up another of his most usually unwanted and irrelevant factoids. But this one had much more of an impact than he could have ever imagined, at least on me.

Did any of us know that the Fleetwood Mac album *Bare Trees* from a few years ago contained a song titled "Dust" and used specific lines from the poem as lyrics? That, at first, threatened to put far more focus on the poem than I could have handled, and I started to plan how I could escape from this room just like I did from study hall, testing my seemingly new resolve about desiring the unobtainable. I focused hard on the Orpheus stairwell girl yet again, and her thighs, and her fine hair, as a long shot that I could perhaps win over such a beauty, knowing full well I couldn't, and wouldn't, and I wanted her to stay forever unobtainable anyways. Clearly, she was more than just a sign to get through the class now, and any thought of her at all, however fantastic, was required nonetheless to divert my attention from the subject at hand.

I began to bounce my foot, in a fit of nerve tapping, and twirl my hair, which I had never done before (but which now seemed absolutely necessary), to try and soothe myself, distract myself, do anything at all to keep me from bursting out of the class, because once you have an unusual amount of fear and anxiety coursing through your veins during a Friday afternoon study hall or basement Lit class, which came upon you uncontrollably, you will forever see Adam Lastings when you read or hear "Dust." No matter where you are. And while I didn't fully understand why this was happening to me, I just knew it would keep on happening.

And that's when the twin added that there was perhaps some concern as to whether Fleetwood Mac properly credited Rupert Brooke, or even had to, due to copyright issues, and public domain and such, which miraculously began to shift the discussion away from the poem itself, especially when Plugger yelled, "That sucks!" Someone else then brought up The Jefferson Airplane's "White Rabbit" and *Alice's Adventures in Wonderland*, and then Led Zeppelin, Tolkien, and The Stones'

"Sympathy for the Devil" along with Baudelaire and Mikhail Bulgakov. Eric Clapton and Cream's cover of Robert Johnson's "Cross Road Blues," and the surrounding myth of Johnson's Faustian pact with the devil, soul for talent, followed, and, thankfully, the discussion did indeed successfully leave Rupert Brooke behind, a much wider discourse about the role of literature and legend in modern culture emerging, this time including books and movies, examples being tossed about in the room as freely as a Friday afternoon intramural football. Who knew which, if any, of the references were actually true, but it didn't matter, it was the discussion itself that mattered most, and I was up for any truth that was up for grabs and not necessarily absolute. If there was a chance that something wasn't as always thought, leading to a potentially different outcome, I was all in.

Much to his credit, our teacher, Mr. Ungerer, let the discussion happen. I hid out in the second row, listening intently though not contributing to the discussion at all for as long as I could, still wanting to go home, and, mercifully, the class finally did end. I left as quickly as I could, each hurried step intended to fortify my newfound enlightenment that desiring the unobtainable may very well be my salvation after all, though the appearance of the devil numerous times in our conversation, along with the Orpheus stairwell girl encounter accompanied by Dante, all happening here in Hamden's Hades, did not escape me and perhaps introduced an entirely different kind of fate that might be headed my way.

As I started up the Chevy, however, and even though I was now safely by myself, without anyone to see me, I let go of the class discussion, which had kind of fizzled out anyway towards the end without a satisfying enough conclusion for me, and the impact of the stairwell encounter began to surprisingly waiver a bit as well. I started to perseverate yet again on whether the stairwell incident was as big as it really seemed to be, maybe it was just more of an impetuous, subconscious attempt to sacrifice rather than save. But when that thought started to raise another bout of anxiousness to accompany the realization that that would mean I would have no anchor at all to rely upon, I quickly dismissed it with such an impressive level of denial that I began to relax a little in the surprising self-knowledge that, healthy or not, I could decide what to believe in, and stick with it, and that made me think of Chloe once again, and how I admired her for her ability to decide things on her own. And maybe that was what Mom did, too, when she needed to get through her days. Maybe she had her own canon of behavior she developed and employed day in and day out, however rough or easy, to get her to the end of her day. Who cares if denial is involved? It's everyone for him or herself, once your guardian angel starts to fall.

I may have very well learned the most important thing I ever would while at Hamden—not from any teacher, or linebacker, or academically superior, dizygotic siblings who admirably never claimed any connection with celebrities, hockey or otherwise, by the way, but from my most perplexing mother. You might think it was how to survive, but it was more crucial than that. The how was up to me. That you *must* survive came from her. My heroic, adult, and, yes, equally unbreakable mother.

Probably the best thing about the end of Lit class, besides it being the end of Lit class, was that it was the end of our poetry module, and I was only too happy to sweep away that dust, so to speak. But I knew it wasn't going to go away easily. I needed the whole weekend to try and understand what had happened to me in study hall that day, why it really did happen, and will it always happen—the next time I'd be in study hall, the next time I'd read a poem? I was pretty sure I could figure it all out between Friday afternoon and Monday morning and force the whole episode out of my mind, as if it never happened, or do whatever it took to not remember it. I thought about telling either my mother or father about it—maybe I should see a doctor because my heart was beating so fast and I was sweaty—but I dismissed that as not at all necessary since my heart always seemed to return to normal, eventually. And, quite honestly, I was a bit scared to have it looked into any further.

I stayed pretty quiet during the weekend, and I tried to sleep as much as possible to block out any lingering fears about the study hall episode. But it kept occurring to me that whatever happened to me in study hall was indeed eerily similar to what happened to me on the field with Chloe, which I had always attributed to a questionable pizza topping, but I had to recognize that it might not have had anything at all to do with our salty garnish of choice. Yet the study hall still seemed far more intense than the field, even though Chloe was someone I had lost, and Adam was someone I hadn't yet fully found. There was a big difference between the two that wasn't adding up—they were both losses: remembered forever, then gone for good. Crimson boughs. And a guy with anxiety and a vexing vocabulary can only take so many of those.

Maybe it was more the place than the person. It seemed like a loss in an open evening field might be processed somewhat differently because it was a place you chose to be in, and that's not at all the same as processing a loss in the confines of a study hall room that belonged to a school that you so desperately wanted to be completely and without question fully disassociated from. But I didn't know.

At least Chloe was still around somewhere, even if I'd never see her again though there was always a chance that I could. There was no chance with Adam. He might have been the one slim hope that I could perhaps finally have changed at Hamden by accepting his friendship, if I wanted to, of course. But I made my choice. And I didn't know if that was the biggest thing about Adam's death, or the fact that his death made Hamden real regardless of what I chose. Either way, something almost tangible would always be with me, an eternal reminder of the place my father hoped, in his heart of hearts, would define me, even and still up to his death many years later.

It did define me, all right, but not for the reason he hoped. I was with Adam out on a field, and he was alive, just like me, just like all of us, and then he wasn't, and I knew then, and forever will know, someone who would never experience from that day forward every big and little thing that my classmates and I would experience by just going on living. He would only know what it was like to be a seventeen-year-old kid, before everything stopped for him.

Every time I thought about that my heart started pounding again. I didn't know what to do about it. I wondered how my father would have handled it. He knew how to handle a lot. He did handle a lot. I was not my father; I am not my father. He too is a hero; I am not. That, too, has defined me.

On Sunday, I thought I should stop worrying about my pounding heart and sense of impending doom that always accompanied it for a while and start looking over upcoming homework. We were given an assignment in Lit class to write something about current events for the next module on realism in literature and I needed to get started. It could be anything: an essay, a story, a poem (God forbid—no poems, my poem for Chloe notwithstanding); it could be about any individual, hero, or victim, large in stature, or tiny yet powerful, or about anything else. We could choose.

I decided to stay as far away from poetry as possible, and I chose to write a play. I wasn't exactly sure what prompted me to do so, surely there must have been some inspiration, maybe I was just getting used to the idea of making my own choices. I considered dramatizing Richard Nixon's break in, for a brief moment, and how a presidential figure can unwittingly intertwine with one's sexual endeavors with a very delightful, southern girl, but I wisely dismissed that idea when I realized

I'd probably have to reference Spiro Agnew somewhere along the way and, well, that would've just made the whole thing quite silly. With enough characters in the news to choose from, I wondered instead what it must be like for just an average person going off to fight in the still ever-present and contentious Vietnam War, someone who wanted to fly under the radar a bit and not be in the lime-light should they end up being thrust into a situation that they couldn't handle.

Suppose it was a person who was just enjoying their life, right where they were, expecting to always be there, when suddenly Bam! Malebolge (once again)! they're whisked away to a place, with no say in the whisking, by someone or some event with power over them to change their life, and then they are forced to adjust the best they can, even though their best may not be good enough. Then I thought that maybe the person might not at first realize that perhaps the change would be good for them, maybe they'd adjust, maybe they'd give it a try and have a little faith, but I was torn as to which side to represent.

When I started writing, it just kind of flowed out that I could do both parts, if they were brothers, if they decided to split to different places and for far different reasons: one to Vietnam, one to Canada (or maybe California?), and this idea seemed to take off, how each one could engage in opposite causes, one by force, one by choice. I guess both were ultimately a choice, the two splitting up, growing up, even if it meant they would never, ever, be the same again—ever, and even if they were close for a brief, youthful moment, the same person, both liking the same things: climbing an apple tree, running through a big ole' empty field on a summer day when no one else is around and you have the whole field to yourself ... and your brother ... and the crickets and the birds are the only things you both hear— and you both do hear them together—and you think those for-ever cherished sounds gotta register to each of you both the same way so that you will always remember those days, and you'll never be apart, or be different, running through those fields that were, well, just like the open field at the end of our street in West Holland Heights, where the road and the sidewalk ran out until they could build some more houses and extend the concrete and asphalt, but until then you had the run of the place, sometimes just the two of you, seeing how far out you could go before one of you might get scared that you were too far from home and couldn't see the houses anymore for the tall weeds. But the other one was just old enough to convince you to keep going anyway, and you were both as one, and you were young, and when you're out in a big summer field with your brother, even if it was only that one time, that's the only place you ever want to be.

I stayed with the play pretty much all Sunday night and most of the next week. I had never spent so much time on any homework assignment before, even on math, which always had the heaviest workload, and which might have been a little easier to concentrate on if Hamden's hockey ace wasn't also in that class. I didn't really know why I all of a sudden started thinking about Plugger, but I was pretty sure I needed to think of anything I could to keep from thinking about Adam, and Chloe, and my heart, and my worry that when big things start happening to me, I get very nervous.

I didn't know why that was, or why I always thought about it, even when trying to write a play that you would think would be consuming enough to block all that stuff out, so maybe thinking about Plugger being in my math class for a bit wasn't such a bad distraction.

I chose without any hesitation at all to recall the day Pounders had sent us all up to the board, like he did every day, and barked out a problem, like he did every day, and we were to write the formula down on the board and try and solve it. Like we did every day. This was usually pretty intimidating at first, but once you got into it and realized everybody was at about the same speed you soon forgot you were up there, and you certainly weren't alone, and you just started working. That one morning, as we all went up, Pounders started to read out the question of the day: one plane takes off from New York on Monday morning, heading east at 600 mph. Another plane takes off from New York on Monday at noon, heading west, and flying at 800 mph. Compensating for the international date line and time zones, and all that navigational and time warp stuff, what day will the two planes meet?

Without missing a beat, while disrupting everyone's concentration, Plugger called out definitively, and with great self-satisfaction at having the answer, "Doomsday!" which was not a bad response at all, drawing spontaneous laughter, and even catching the cranky Pounders by surprise, while introducing the up until then foreign notion that perhaps Plugger was cerebrally capable after all, albeit highly limited (though every one of his intellectual observations was customarily accompanied by the apparent need to bellow inappropriately, which failed miserably to underscore any of his pronouncements with any level of academic authority whatsoever).

Any assignments in classes I had with Plugger—and there were a few, including Lit, which I started to believe were payback for my athletic abstention—required an extra effort of concentration on my part to succeed and avoid any resultant, vodka-related wrath, and I found it quite ironic that I needed to concentrate deeply in classes with Plugger to avoid his distractions, yet those same distractions were all of a sudden desperately required to help me stop concentrating so much on my worrisome state of mind, and return me to the task at hand: my play. And just when you think a guy like Plugger would never add any value to your academic life whatsoever—and he didn't—he nonetheless gave me something with his playful, aviation-based response on that occasion. And I gotta tell you, I would never have expected appreciating our hockey ace under any circumstances whatsoever but thinking of him and his antics was not half bad, all of a sudden, and, I have to admit, he calmed my mind at times, if only through recollection, not actual interaction, but sometimes that's all you need when you're trying to settle yourself from calamities and focus on writing a play. I loved writing that play.

I was pretty quiet in the car on the drive to school the day the assignment was due, and throughout all my other classes that preceded Lit class that day as well. I was also beginning to feel a little nauseous, quite nervous that maybe my play wasn't going to be that good after all. Maybe when Mr. Ungerer said that we were free to write anything he didn't mean anything. Maybe his version of anything had boundaries. Everything does—you can't just go along doing whatever you want, you'll get slapped down, surely you will, if you whip out a dictionary for patriarchal, corrective purposes, for example, or don't follow the mathematically oriented path you're expected to.

Finally, after dawdling as much as humanly possible right beforehand, I went into Lit class and sat in the back. We handed over our papers as Mr. Ungerer, sporting his usual bow tie and white, baggy, wrinkly shirt that looked like it had no idea that there was such a thing as an ironing board that it might want to befriend, went up and down the aisle collecting them, mumbling observations to himself and looking genuinely interested in what each student had interpreted as "anything." He was remarkably relaxed, his usual facial tick of fast-blinking eyes peculiarly at bay as he seemed to take pleasure in each of the paper's titles, giving him an indication as to just how inventive each paper potentially might be.

As he approached me, my heart began to pound a bit yet again. I just wanted him to take my paper from me, stick it in the middle of the stack, and move on—I was getting a little sick and tired of being afraid of my heart pounding so frequently since Adam died. I was beginning to think that maybe I should tell Mom about my heart and go see a doctor after all when a ruckus occurred just as Mr. Ungerer stopped in front of me.

The classroom door had opened and Plugger came in late, apparently still talking to some other kid in the hall even as he came through the door. As unacademically decorated as he was, Plugger nonetheless was rarely late to any class, starting with early morning algebra, courtesy of a small, decorative, and critically functional cactus plant strategically placed in close enough proximity to the snooze button on his nightstand clock radio (by a very committed mother indeed) to ensure punctuality, however puncturing at that. (The year-end certificate awarding perfect attendance would be his if Plugger's mother had anything to do with it. And she did, desperate to snag something, anything, of recognized authority, documenting at least effort, if certainly not results, for any potential college to consider, should they even elect to open any long-shot envelopes containing Plugger's application.)

But there must have been quite an altercation in the hallway as Plugger entered the classroom because he wasn't fully committed to the class just yet, if that was ever even possible for him. As he grabbed the chair in the very last row that was next to both mine and the door, he turned to the hallway, and in what was clearly an expression devoid of even a hint of any social filter whatsoever, though arguably perhaps the single most memorable and identifiable Hamden moment that could have made my entire experience there finally worth all the aggravation, he got up to close the door and he yelled out forcibly into the hallway at the mysterious protagonist, "Eat me!" while quite emphatically grabbing his most clearly undesirable family jewels with his hockey-dominant left hand, offering up neither a take-out delicacy for immediate sustenance nor a treasure trove of coveted, genetic superiority.

In one continuous motion, Plugger then closed the door and turned to Mr. Ungerer, who gasped, hand to mouth while blinking his eyes in almost uncontrollable, rapid-fire fashion, and Plugger said to the fragile, flustered faculty member, most sincerely and once again without missing a beat, "Sorry, sir, here's my paper." And Plugger sat down, quite relaxed, holding out his work, however queasily, with the same hand that only moments ago had challenged the dignity of some poor, hallway slob. He then waited quite contentedly for Mr. Ungerer's approach, Plugger giving the class his full attention now, as much as possible with him, as if nothing at all had just happened. Nothing at all.

All that commotion would certainly remove any attention whatsoever from my paper, I was sure, suddenly convinced that Mr. Ungerer would mechanically, and blindly, just take it from me while he figured out how to recover from his most embarrassing display of ineptitude in dealing with the profane, inept, and, once again, despite school policy, visibly bearding left winger. But just as I was feeling grateful that a classmate yet again came to my rescue to divert attention from my anxiety-ridden presence, albeit this time nowhere near as poignantly appreciated as the twin's study hall and even earlier Lit class Fleetwood Mac efforts, my gratitude was short lived. I guess everything happens for a reason.

My paper seemed to serve Mr. Ungerer with just the perfect distraction he desperately needed because he stopped in front of me far longer than he did at anyone else's desk, and far, far longer than I wanted him to. I thought he was mustering the courage to engage the suddenly, and disturbingly, orally prolific Plugger, sitting regrettably right next to me, but Mr. Ungerer's face had now changed, the blinking slowed dramatically, he ran his hand through his hair, leaving it in a most noticeably unsettled state when he finished, and he regained his composure. "Hmm, a play," he said to himself, eyes still on my paper, his mumble both loud and soft enough for us to know that he didn't realize anyone else could hear him. And when a teacher says "Hmm ..." in reference to your work, it generally isn't a bad thing.

He kept reading my first page as he continued on and approached Plugger, Mr. Ungerer now safely preoccupied and no longer at all threatened by the potential for more hallway gems. He held his hand out in desperate hope of a fluke masterpiece from the hockey player, still never lifting his eyes from my work, or commenting on the crinkled mess that was presented to him instead by Plugger's most unwelcome left hand, however blood free (unlike the early morning algebra assignments not so fortuitously far enough removed from Plugger's prickly wake ups), so, thanks to the comment that metaphorically sucked all the attention out of the room at what became the exact right time, I was pretty sure the "Hmm" was all I would get, and that was plenty for me.

I went home that day, feeling pretty good about the play and the acceptable amount of low-profile attention it received, despite being uncomfortably intermingled with an understandable level of intrigue surrounding the identity of the intended recipient of Plugger's challenge for immediate oral gratification, no Christian male or female first name having been offered during the outburst. (Despite the two young Winthrop women in the class, one of whose laughter at the incident was a highly unexpected, considering her quite diminutive stature, single, mega horn-like blast, followed by stunning silence, and despite the high probability of more Winthropian women roaming the hallways at any given moment, it was undoubtedly clear by his reckless tone and disturbing volume that the unguarded, blunt force of Plugger's outburst, without any sensitive, charm-like pleading whatsoever, cut the gender possibility of the mystery awardee necessarily in half. Identification by male name would surely follow at some point. It never did.)

When the next Lit class came around that week, I discovered that Mr. Ungerer was not through with me yet. He had made copies of my play. And he passed them out. He passed them out! I thought at first that it was an assignment of required, in-class reading of some famous authorial work, but then I got my copy and saw the title.

"Let's all take a look at Mr. Skully's play," Mr. Ungerer said, with an unusual calm authority, and with no nervous tics this time at all. "This is a nice interpretation of the assignment," he went on. "Read it over tonight. Then I think we should use the stage in the auditorium during class on Thursday and run through it. A rehearsal only. We'll talk then about who will play which part. Nice job, Mr. Skully."

Shit. That was more attention than I ever wanted. I said nothing in response as we moved on, but I have to admit, I wasn't totally upset about it. Mr. Ungerer went on to explain that we were just going to enact the play on the stage for only us, no one else, just an exercise to see how it would look. I kind of liked that. I did not want any attention that would bring in an audience to see something that I did only because I had to, though found out that I liked anyway, but still wanted to keep mostly to myself. But I could settle for a "rehearsal only."

Thursday finally came and the class gathered in the auditorium, and it felt strange to be somewhere different than a classroom because of something I had done. I suddenly longed for my seat in the back row of room 102 in the garden basement, which, while somewhat undesirable, was familiar nonetheless, and I always craved familiarity so I wouldn't feel out of place anywhere, or any time, in Hamden, especially at that moment. Mr. Ungerer had not yet told me what role I would play, though I assumed he'd let me read one of the brother's lead parts, which I did not want to do—I did not want at all to hear my voice in the Hamden auditorium, speaking words I wrote that would be audible to others who might be passing by thereby further cementing my role as a student in Hamden who might be once again remembered for something. What if he decides to put the play on for others after all, I thought, under growing stress; what if it makes the yearbook? It already may be entering the memory of every kid in class, and I didn't even want that.

But then Mr. Ungerer did an astonishing thing. He started with stage directions, putting the actors in place, pitting the two brothers against each other, and then he said, "Mr. Skully, come back here with me." Much to my surprise, I went to sit with him, several rows deep into the auditorium, to see how the play would look from the seats.

I was surprised that I wasn't going to be in it, but Mr. Ungerer actually did a damn good thing by having me sit with him and watch as the play unfolded, transforming before me from the solitary work I had done in the comfort of being alone in my bedroom, one weekend, to a piece of work being performed by others, it now leaving me entirely and belonging to my class-mates onstage to deliver in a most appealing fashion. I was both nervous and stunned to see something I had dreamed up on my own now in the hands of guys I had been trying to mysteriously distance myself from and would, nonetheless, continue to do so afterwards, despite the trust placed in their hands to deliver the play.

And they did deliver, taking it seriously, working the dia-logue, adding depth. Some of the guys who were also in the drama club added a flair and intensity I hadn't realized existed when I wrote the piece.

Had I been onstage delivering lines in my most unadorned, droning voice, making it nothing more than a mechanical as-signment, I might not have seen it in the necessary and dis-sociative manner that would bring it to life.

And had I not been seated next to Mr. Ungerer while all this was going on, I would have missed the experience of him tapping me on the arm and saying while the play continued onstage, "I think you should be a writer, think about it. I have a novel that you might like, it's full of imagination that shows what you can do when you really let go. Stop by this afternoon."

He then got up, went to the stage, gave a few more directions, and asked them to run through it again. While he said that, the actors gathered around and began making more suggestions, talking about what might work better, what they liked, what they didn't like. The whole thing took on an even bigger life than it did just moments ago when I had heard the words that were only meant to come from my pen, and not be heard by anyone else—ever, coming out of somebody else indeed!

Just as Mr. Ungerer then turned to look at me from the stage, in a frozen, timeless moment, with a further confirmation of his desire that I consider being a writer by conveying a quick look of 'see what can happen,' which I'm sure he thought only he and I would be privy to, Plugger yelled out from the back of the stage. He, thankfully, had not been trusted with any dialogue whatsoever, but the beginnings of his raised voice had the whole room collectively holding their breath for a potential sequel to his Monday morning vivid, if not somewhat vaudevillian, vituperation of sorts.

"Hey, Shakespeare, I like this!" he bellowed out, his loud voice causing the diminutive coed to snicker to herself in memory of his rather earthy, early-week explosion. I got up impulsively and headed out of the auditorium, desperately looking for a water fountain (or any reason at all to leave and gather myself so as to slow my always now-racing heart, especially of late whenever any Hamden-based attention was thrown my way) when Plugger added. "Where the hell are you going?"

Remarkably, Mr. Ungerer did not ask me to come back; he let me go. He must have oddly known I needed a moment to myself, trusting that I would be back once he noticed a fountain within earshot, and he corralled everyone else and had them go through the play one more time, despite the study-hall-locker twin's reply to Plugger's Shakespeare reference by insisting he saw a blend of Eugene O'Neill and Tennessee Williams much more so than the famous English playwright and bard. He could even see volumes of personal encyclopedic work in my future, the twin went on, not unlike *Naturalis Historia*, courtesy of a personal favorite ancient Roman of his, Pliny the Elder (though he was quick to point out the merits of the Younger as well, castigating neither one for their possible involvement in the roman numeral scheme), providing, of course, that I was willing to dictate to servants while taking a bath, the twin choosing, of all possible details, The Elder's supposed writing style, which created an immediate awkward silence upon its utterance, but an opportunity for others to break that silence.

"What about James Baldwin?" someone offered.

"My favorite James is Agee," another said.

"Let Us Now Praise Famous Men!" echoed yet another, specifying the celebrated Agee piece.

"Isn't that what we're doing?" Plugger asked, visibly confused and not paying too much attention.

"Jane Austen!" someone then said.

"The Bronte sisters!" one of the girls shouted.

"Why are we shouting out names?" someone asked.

"Hey! Let's praise famous women too—we should read those brontosaurus sister books," Plugger said, his surprisingly admirable stance for equality taking a wrong turn at the last minute, as all his oral renderings so frequently did. I was grateful the Orpheus stairwell girl was not in this class.

"Yes, we should!" the twin added, referring to the call for female praise and not the Late Jurassic period literary treats that Plugger apparently unearthed all on his own. "Let's start with Zora Neale Hurston and her under-appreciated masterpiece, *Their Eyes Were Watching God*, he continued authoritatively, clearly enthused by the discussion and the attention the "rehearsal only" was bringing to his personal intellectual favorites from his own reading list, not Hamden's, which Mr. Ungerer curiously let him continue to offer, suspiciously in the context of 'see what can happen.'

Mr. Ungerer was pretty damn good at letting conversations continue, and so the twin did, adding that I might want to read the Hurston book to appreciate a character's growth from innocence to adulthood, though the circumstances are quite different. But the impact from facing a desperate life or death choice regarding someone you love, and for your own salvation, is most certainly universal and could work for the brothers in my play, he argued, though I had no idea what he was talking about, still at the water fountain, far enough away yet rewardingly close enough to pick up the whole conversation without revealing my interest.

But the twin always knew what he was talking about, and he introduced me to deeper levels of consideration when all I wanted, dammit, was to write a play. And I didn't know how the hell referencing two classic, American playwrights could lead one down a road to multi-generational, ancient Roman intellectuals, other more contemporary intellectuals, and then a most gifted writer who possibly shunned, at first, a large movement like the Harlem Renaissance because she wanted to deal first with human issues, regardless of the color of the packaging, as the twin defended one school of thought on the matter. I'm sure the twin was only trying to further support me, which he seemed to do most frequently after seeing me and Adam out on the field, but he was clearly being ridiculously over complementary through his love of arcane knowledge, and I think everyone at Hamden, teachers included, gave up long ago trying to keep up with the minds of either one of the twins.

But I had to admit it, introducing me to a writer who may have wanted to steer clear of any bigger issues and just write their story was another damned nice gift he gave me. How the hell did he know to do those things? And while it might be quite intimidating to sit next to someone as smart as he was under normal circumstances, once that someone starts doing things for you, well, it's really not so bad.

I sipped the water from the fountain slowly, elongating my time alone in the hall. I was hoping to ease my stubborn shaking at the thought of the play soaring away from me, being treated with respect by my classmates (and ancient Romans alike), and being noticed by a teacher with a distinctive name, who wore ridiculous bow ties and perpetually wrinkled clothes, who had a nervous tic and a most assuredly non-commanding presence about him, who I didn't know that well, who let kids talk, and who took me aside and took a risk right smack in the middle of the day by seating me in the perfect place to make sure I would see the bigger picture of how something I produced was happening in front of me. He could have put me onstage where I would have missed everything.

It was a damned nice thing he did for me (dammit, both he and the twin at the same time) though, again, I did not like anyone at Hamden doing anything nice for me. I was momentarily conflicted, once again, about yet another possible new opportunity for me, not unlike a Friday with Adam, or an evening in a field with Chloe, or even a breast-pressed-to-palm moment with Nathalie, though none of those ended well, or took me to a better place that I could see at the moment. But this new "opportunity" was in an area in which I didn't know I had any talent, and I undoubtedly revealed to at least Mr. Ungerer, if not others as well, that my desperate attempts to hide from life in Hamden were apparently more visible to others than I ever realized. It made me nervous that Mr. Ungerer apparently saw that in me, enough to put my play, and me, on display in a way that he might have hoped would've brought me along, or broke through my shell, but it only served to further awaken my anxiety levels when I thought that the only other adult who had any other strong opinion about what I should do with my life was my father. And there was no water fountain anywhere that would allow me to walk away from how that was playing out. So, it didn't take long for me to dislike Mr. Ungerer for introducing me to a part of myself that I didn't know was out there (but was most likely unfulfillable anyway), and for trying to help me by putting me in a position to possibly make my own choice about my future, that choice really being far bigger and more important than choosing to write one lousy play for a homework assignment.

Once we finished with the play, I found a way to hurry off to the next class before anyone could tell me that they liked it, if indeed they really did, but they did, I knew it. They did. A lot. My nervous heart was proof. They liked it just enough for me to make my decision that I would write no more plays and stray no further from the logical boundaries of an assignment ever again. If I even tried to continue writing, I convinced myself, I might actually like it, and then I'd be back in an all too familiar conundrum, just like with Chloe, even Adam, and distracted again from why I was sent to Hamden to begin with. And after everything that had happened, it was pretty clear that I was no good at conundrums. So, there were at least two things I now knew that I just couldn't, or wouldn't, do anymore: bang delightful Southern girls who inspire poems without titles and bang out equally delightful, sibling-based plays, again without a title. And that said everything about who I was. And who I am. Though you can probably find a title for that: loser.

Later that day, despite my resolve, I still picked up that book about that Columbian family, with all that imagination in it, from Mr. Ungerer, which wasn't a play at all like he said but was still something that could dangerously further my interest in writing. I hated Mr. Ungerer for dangerously furthering my interest in writing. I'll never read it, I convinced myself, I have enough trouble keeping up with the Hamden reading list, and now I have this? Not to mention gems from the twin? God, I hated Hamden. I quickly tucked the book neatly into a secure spot in my backpack, so it wouldn't get damaged, but mostly to not be noticed by others. I hurried off to my next class in plenty of time to review the assignment from the night before and be fully prepared and within expected boundaries, as I am always expected to be.

As junior year finally started to wind down, the choice of college was going to be taken even more seriously in the upcoming fall, which meant I could no longer ignore that underlying, pressing, however yet unspoken, directive that engineering was going to be in my future in much the same way that Hamden was. Whenever I walked down the hall near the classroom where I'd be taking trigonometry next year, I always felt an almost imperceptible chill run down my spine at the Scrooge-like glimpse of yet another Ghost of Something Yet to Come (or eerie grandfatherly) long, bony finger beckoning, this time it being engineering, nothing peppermint-sweet about that. But that classroom was also near the auditorium, and whenever I got close to it, I'd grab a quick drink at my favorite fountain of not-to-be-cherished-prep-school youth, right outside of it (and serving the best damn water to ever quench even the tiniest fire, however promising). Then I'd peek inside at the plaque now permanently affixed to the wall in memory of one Adam Lastings.

Enough months had elapsed by May of junior year such that Adam faded into the distance of the collective memory of Hamden; no one could afford to remember him, there was too much pressure to define the next phase of life. We would all leave this place in about twelve months, but Adam wouldn't. He was forever seventeen years old, somewhere, and once we walked out the door, we would never see that plaque again, or think of him in the absolute shocking, yet numbing, and impressionable way we did when we, too, were seventeen and first heard the news that one of us, just as old as us, just as scared as us, just as full of life as some of us, was gone.

We were instructed to pay sincere tribute to Adam, and we did, and everything stopped during a lost week, which was fully supported by all the adults above us, especially the parents, whose collective deep breath mixing genuine, crushing sorrow, but frightful relief that it wasn't their child, and the guilt that accompanies two such opposing viewpoints held concurrently, could be virtually heard upon their exhale whenever and wherever they showed up on campus. Adam did not have to decide what to do next; there was no engineering in his future. I liked to think that my close brush with his Jeff Spear-like exuberance during his final days stuck to me somewhere in a most positive place, but it most likely lodged in some ventricle that my heart could not properly take in, nor repel, causing all that new-found rapid firing that is not at all how I would have expected a heart to process such a profound experience.

But nothing ever seems to happen the way it's supposed to, and I was convinced that I might very well be stuck with that most uncomfortable piece of Adam imbedded in me for a long time. He had put me to my most severe test, offering me change one more time, and I failed, quite emphatically, further proof coming in Ungerer's class that Adam, and Chloe as well, showed me who I was, and who I was not to be. And I had one more year at Hamden coming up to remind me yet again.

Our last assignment in Lit class during junior year was to write a sample of what we thought our upcoming college application essay should be. It didn't matter which school we'd eventually send it to, we were just to tell a little about ourselves, hand it in on the last day of class, and Mr. Ungerer would hold onto them and give them to our senior year Lit class teacher in September (if it wasn't him), after we had a whole summer to mull it over. We would then get the essays back on the first day of class senior year and rewrite them, eventually tailoring them to the schools to which we would apply, which was a most perplexing assignment. I wasn't sure I wanted to reveal what I had come to know about myself, and I wondered why any teacher would be so deeply interested in the welfare and next phase of life of a bunch of privileged, adolescent kids, most of whom would soar far above any of the Hamden teachers in their careers, and all of whom most likely would never be seen again after donning caps and gowns and leaving with the requisite sheepskin credentials.

And the whole idea of which college to attend was beginning to generate yet another new level of anxiety in me, and it most assuredly would require a major decision that my father would be a part of (as he had been all along throughout the whole process), and after completing my sentence at Hamden, how could I even begin to fathom the idea of going somewhere else that was planned for me? At least I had the whole summer to work on that part, and since my father was quite preoccupied with the state of the country, most notably the ever-present Watergate scandal, competing for his attention was going to be a bit difficult, which was all right with me.

As I sat down to start the essay, I thought it would be good to consider both a macro observation of the world at large, due to the current political and recent wartime turmoil, and then a micro observation of my own life, and see how those two intersect. That would surely impress any college. So, two things came right to mind that might inform such an approach, the first, once again, being that Nixon's troubles seemed to have annoyingly accompanied my prior summer with Chloe and then threatened to walk me down the aisle of graduation as well, offering both the macro and micro views I was considering. There was no doubt about how disappointingly things ended with Chloe, but could things overall really have gotten any worse in the summer of '74? I was betting good ole' Milhous was gonna come through his troubles okay, which I thought my father was convinced of as well, which would have put my father in a better mood to discuss college and my secret, gnawing desire that I might want to go to school in California, near my brother, instead of here in the east, his idea.

Wasn't exactly sure when and how to approach that topic, if at all, but as long as everything settled down in the news, and things stayed status quo, and Tricky Dick resumed a more normal tenure in the White House, he could very well be open to it, I was convinced. And an all's-well-that-ends-well kind of sensibility would surely exude a mature and optimistic attitude that would indeed impress any college, showing them that no matter how much pesky, presidential improprieties impede upon the pleasures of the procreative process, assuming only pleasure and not pregnancy occur, one can adjust and plow through, so to speak. Certainly, a much-coveted skill for being able to handle schoolwork in the midst of anything else life throws you along the way.

The second thing that occurred to me was that Mr. Ungerer getting us to focus on ourselves in the essay without regard yet to which school we would apply to was, by all accounts, another pretty good thing he did. I was sure some of the other kids were already quite certain where they were going to apply, especially those few who smugly knew Harvard and Yale had already sprung their doors wide open for them, their gasconading cascade of unabashed, brash and brainy blather anything but impressive. Bastards.

But, like I had said, I had a bit of a problem ahead of me on that front, so not worrying about which college to go to was a pretty good thing, at least for me, and it should help keep me focused on my macro-micro idea as well. But, dammit, I did have my fill of Mr. Ungerer doing very admirable things, it only served to rile me up again, and that would not be the best way to start an essay about yourself. But I did start, and it didn't take me very long, it having almost as easy a flow as my play had, and I went and got a soda when I finished, just to let my mind settle, and I sat out in the back yard, directly in the sun, and I drank it down while experiencing the hot sun on my face and the cold liquid pouring down my throat. And I wasn't at all sure which of those two opposite things felt better.

Then I went back up to my room to see what I had written, which ended up being more like a letter than an essay because addressing it directly to somebody like "Dear Admissions Office" of no school in particular really did free me up, surprisingly. I laid on the floor with my letter-essay because I wanted my head as close to the ground as possible, to see if it read any better down where nobody really spends much time.

Almost nobody. And, damn it, after all that planning and all that confident thinking, it turned out I didn't write a damn thing about any clever, nifty intertwining of macro and micro ideas at all. Apparently, the Hamden words to live by, about " ... All Thy Getting ... " somehow snuck in and took control of my pen, and the last thing you want is something from Hamden rearing its ugly head and applying itself to other aspects of your life because then you'll never get away from that school. But those words found their way in, and they truly informed my letter-essay, even much more so than Mr. Ungerer's guidance to forget about specific colleges. And maybe that's what my father wanted for me all along, to get some understanding, about everything I keep talking about, like my parents, Illinois, Hamden, and, well, my parents. I never knew why I kept talking about them so much, but maybe that's what you do with complicated heroes, you just keep talking so you'll know that they'll know you ultimately love them, especially (but not only) for everything they've given you, things you couldn't possibly see while they were being given but become pretty damn clear after the beginning of the end of something, like Hamden. But, make no mistake, Hamden is no onion field, and regardless of any Ungerer-inspired epiphanies, like I said, I was still living for the day of the Hamden vanishing point, hoping that that day would come relatively soon. But now there was an essay, or a letter, that someone might read, so I thought I had better read it first, and pretty thoroughly at that. And that's exactly what I did:

Dear Admissions Office:

I am Ogden Skully, and I am applying to your school for fall semester, 1975. Here's everything you need to know about me: I like to be alone; I am calm alone; I went to a private High School; I hated it. I don't really know why.

To continue, I am nervous; I want to be safe; i need to be safe. I don't think I can take care of myself yet, but I can play baseball and football, and I am good. I see myself as someone who does not engage in life but observes it and records it internally instead. I am also empathetic to other people's problems, especially to those of Southern girls. That comes from observing and recording. But they can piss me off too. Other people and their problems, that is, not Southern girls, those girls are usually a lot further along than me in terms of life, which can be quite embarrassing, but not enough to piss me off.

Just because I am shy doesn't mean I can't do anything intimately, though, because I think I can write. And I think I might be pretty good at it, even though I won't be writing any more plays and I tend to use long sentences and sound a little overly full of myself at times, believe it or not, which occurs mostly when I am comfortable and relaxed and feeling fairly insulated against anything going wrong. I don't know when those times are. I seem to unwittingly, or perhaps deliberately, represent myself this way, for some reason, and I am most eager to discover why, which I could very well do while strolling your most appealingly lush campus quad.

In addition to writing, it might help you to know that I'm pretty good at my other schoolwork, too; I get good grades. And I test well, in school that is. I am good enough at enough things to keep me from being too noticed, though I neverthe-less allow myself to stick my head out of my shell whenever I choose to–a deliberate tortoise of sorts, which, admittedly, can create problems on stairwells in the home, generally. I am still trying to understand things, but this is the principal thing I'm working on: I want to feel malice toward my father for controlling and preplanning my life, and for being too much the faithful consumer of fine spirits, but he suffered so outra-geously when he was young, and he was only doing the best he could, so how could you blame him? I see his other side (I wonder if my brother does).

And, let's face it, feeling "malice toward none" might be a lot better than feeling malice toward anyone, as Honest Abe so insightfully stated, though he may not have realized at the time that he was describing both Chloe's quite generous ac-ceptance of the male gender at large and my internal turmoil about my father. Plus, there was that time at Hamden when my father stood up for me. And once, come to think of it, I wrote a story that he actually liked and showed around to some of his colleagues at work, though I think he was most comfortable assuming writing was just a hobby that wouldn't interfere with his plans for my future. This was after I decided I wouldn't write any more plays, but stories didn't count. Yet.

But those things he did really stuck with me. I never told anyone about that until right now. And there were a few other things he did for me, scattered among the things he did to me, so I really have no reason to hate, right? I find the weight of all of this most debilitating. The frustration doesn't allow me to point my anger anywhere, or to grow, unless I take charge of myself and make a decision as to how I feel, which would be most exonerating, but I don't do things like that.

Allow me to persevere; I am perplexed by my mother. She was very tortured about marrying my father, I know that, but she went ahead with it anyway. He oppressed her mightily in our alcoholic house, but I think they stayed together because they were both still looking for a rainbow of sorts. To net out my conclusion about her: I don't know her; I never had a deep conversation with her because she never seemed happy enough for that, but I'm thinking now that that may be more my fault than hers. After all, how often is an anxiety-ridden, self-described, sociopathic-loner-teenager the first person a mother thinks of when she needs to talk, regardless of how superb a college candidate that desirable teenager most certainly may be. I kinda think I do know her; I just don't know me very well, surprising as that may sound.

I sometimes think that she wasn't there for me in the way I needed her most, though, emotionally, that is. And let's face it; I wasn't there for her either, though my brother certainly was, at a most critical time, no less, even if it took a while for me to figure that out. Yet she was there for me in many functional ways, which freed me from realizing at the time that I needed her emotionally. Within this conundrum she afforded me the luxury of not having to be aware of some very important, gaping holes until I would be old enough to handle them. I don't know when that will be (no further details will be forthcoming on that topic). I could be angry with her for being a conundrum type of mother, but I see her other side.

And she pretty much showed all her sides, however mysterious (though certainly brave, which she still is), and that has to be worth something. Don't you think?

I find the weight of all of this most debilitating. She is quite nervous and I'm thinking I may be more like her than my father; I may be her, in fact, though she is undoubtedly far braver than me, and you have to recognize that real bravery is a lonely thing to be burdened with. But, like I said, I know her now; I just don't know me. But this now makes sense. And if you're thinking, "Why don't I just forgive both of them and move on?" well, it's not at all that simple. You don't forgive someone for being who they are and doing the best they can, especially when maybe something they *didn't like made* them who *they* are. *That would make you a pretentious kind of jerk to think that a person needs to be excused for the person they are. You have to do something else that has nothing to do with forgiveness. I'm not sure what that is, though. Much is still unknown. I wish I could ask my brother about all this.*

I have to admit that I am tired of going over and over this information, as if each new turn will reveal something new. It very well may, but it may not lead to any life changing actions. In my experience, even when things like a bright, new morning comes first (though I am not at all a morning student, Mr. Pounders' quite ripe classroom notwithstanding), the day always ends in the same darkness. But maybe just living is life changing enough. I'll continue to contemplate these things, hopefully within the hallowed hallways of your most academically respected institution.

I guess, in summary, I'm a little worried that I fail to grow up when it counts (no further details will be forthcoming on this topic). But don't worry, even though I plan on remaining mad at everything and everybody connecting me to Hamden, despite any enlightenment I may have discovered, I won't let any foolish fustigations on my part interfere with my school-work. I never did at Hamden.

In closing, I am excited to hopefully experience everything your exceptional ivory tower has to offer, from the highest levels of academic study to, in your case, I'm quite certain, despite that recent Times article on questionable college food programs in general, your most delicious and highly nutrition-ally balanced meal plan options. I hope you agree that by this introduction you need look no further than this letter-essay for the model, incoming freshman student you so selectively seek. I must confess, though. I may have lied (just a tad, mind you) when writing all of this, though I'm not exactly certain about which parts in particular. I have been known to do that on occasion, though it has never really changed the truth.

And please excuse the use of three pronouns not in italics in that one sentence somewhere above. I realize now that it may look to you like I don't think you are clever enough to understand exactly to whom I was referring. I, most assuredly, intended nothing of the sort; it just helps me a great deal to overly emphasize whenever I write about the people who made me who I am. I am every one of them.

Lastly, please don't let any of the above admissions negatively influence my chance for admission. I have kept this deliberately brief for your benefit, but I can further expound if required. I look forward to your reply with great confidence.

Yours truly,

Ogden Skully

Turned out to be a fortuitous decision to be on the floor. It was always such a comforting place to be, even when you were about to read a letter but got distracted by looking under your bed, which was quite dust-free and lemony-fresh in the far reaches where a mother never missed with the mop, and where I used to hide on occasion back before my brother left. He and our father would get into arguments, pretty bad ones, especially that last one in the kitchen, directly below my room. They yelled so loud behind the closed kitchen door—there was a lot of noise down there.

Then my brother left. Our mother was on the other side of that door, banging on it as if she were knocking for permission to enter, even though the door had no lock on it, and my brother left.

The next day there was a good size drop, like a nickel, left behind on the kitchen floor, dry, red. I still don't know how she missed that. I didn't, but then again, that was about the time her own drinking was discovered, glasses suddenly left in the sink, redolent of the overnight, pale perfume of the liquor of choice in our house, paired curiously with root beer, Kool-Aid, and anything else that was available. I guess she was getting so desperate for her own form of safety that she didn't care who knew what about her anymore, including the pills that came after. And that was my mother in bits and pieces, yet again.

But I gotta say, to this day, even though my brother left us and found his way out to California to free himself from continued combat with the vodka-king (only, thankfully, and not the Viet Cong too, due to his mercifully high draft number—two unpopular, unwinnable wars would have been too much for any confused, hurt, and angry offspring to endure), he actually did a pretty good thing: he saved our mother by not subjecting her nerves to any more visions of her older son continuing to fight in the house she had found for us when we improved our lives by moving to Eden Falls, Connecticut.

Even if he never really came back to us, he saved her when she didn't yet know that that was one of the times when she needed it most, sometime during my stay at Hamden and before I couldn't save her again out on the lawn, though I'm still not sure she could see what he had done for her through the foggy lens of her sorrow at his leaving, and the bravery of her staying. In the process, though, he eventually found his safety.

My safety back then, and even further back in West Holland Heights, was under my bed, and then just lying on the floor near it when I started to get a little too big for that sort of thing. I liked to feel the security of all that properly sealed, polyurethane finished, hardwood support under more of me than just my feet, which was something I would have never admitted to anyone. Except maybe Chloe.

I liked being under my bed best, though. It was clean and tight and dark under there, and … safe, kind of like being buried alive. It was a good place to be, and where I learned not to get into any fights with my father. I should've thanked my brother for that. I never did. To tell you the truth, though, I didn't mind feeling buried at all, as long as it involved the people whose pain made me who I still am. Yes, I am every one of them—another fatal flaw—which was kind of a bombshell to discover, and to put in a letter-essay to no one in particular way back then, but not so much now. And even though you wrote all those letter-essay words down for someone else to read, they still sneaked up on you as some kind of personal wisdom when you were flat on your back, on a freshly waxed floor, proofreading that completely stupid college draft that wasn't the one you handed in but the one you kept anyway. And still read even now.

It's always a good idea to put a bombshell in writing and keep the words close by. You'll want to read them over and over again, and every time you relive things like Hamden Academy, and indoor iron railings, and losing things like brothers, girlfriends, neighborhoods, cultural identities, kids named Adam, and general innocence overall, though that's still up for debate. But you still relive it all. Because all you're trying to do is pinpoint exactly when you first knew whom you would always be. No matter how embarrassingly long that may take. So you could understand the choices you might make throughout your life. Or might not.

Like whether you should have never let a steamy, open field stop you from a second chance; whether you should have said, "the hell with it," and started a teenaged, French revolution of your own kind, palms up and raring to go; whether you should have said, "the hell with it," yet again, and told a Hamden kid with freckles and a sensibility you could trust that you, too, had a girlfriend that went to another school; whether you should have lived the words, "the hell with it," and drove a victimized, mysterious, dedicated, uniquely strong, though momentously sad, mother away from her own inferno to find her own Orpheus moment, never, never, looking back; whether you should have gone to UCLA after Hamden, where you really wanted to go, though that discussion doesn't go nearly as planned, especially when Tricky Dick betrays you by resigning at the most inopportune time, when you most desperately need a calm, sober father; whether you should have asked out more girls from that small eastern college you attended instead, fairly certain you would have found one to love eventually, and enough to start a family with; whether you should have written more stories, poems, or plays, at least after your second reading of *One Hundred Years of Solitude*, but certainly long before now.

And whether you should admit that teaching English at that small Connecticut school you've settled into, and as a second language in Manhattan on nights and weekends as well, really isn't all that bad, knowing full well that there's no better gift you can give anyone than words and the music they produce. Not in any Pygmalion-Henry Higgins kind of way, just as something to be put to good use. And no hiding behind them.

Yes, that's all you're trying to do, get an understanding, nothing more. Which, admittedly, can be pretty damn hard to do while you're waiting for everything that might have happened, had there been no vodka to contend with, to grow smaller and disappear and free you at last from such a torturous grip. Which you're mistakenly sure will happen sometime, even if you hold out until the passing of a mother and father who were both remarkably loved, regardless of everything, and who suffered and loved you in earnest to the best of their ability, though that may not have been quite enough. Never is. For anyone.

You're sure there's no alcohol in the world that can out-live those who mishandled it to soothe the fires of their own abuse, but you are wrong. It's always there, in some way. In your hope to be freed from the pain of someone who hero-ically loved you while being so fully diminished, long before you knew they were, you are very wrong, and it seems to me still that the reach of a dark and distant Irish grandfather's hand while clenching a belt and a bottle was indeed so much longer than he could have possibly known, extending further still among even those a couple generations removed, and too affected in their own anxiety-ridden way to pick up the bottle themselves. Though surely that had nothing to do with any courage to break any cycles.

And who knows how far back it all started? Which leaves no vodka villains who aren't victims as well, Grandfather, Father, though there's no full vindication in that. Remembered voice or not.

But you still have to find out how you can move on. You must, as your mother showed. And you knew at that moment, on those crumbly, uneven concrete steps, and with absolute certainty, what was going to keep you safe for the rest of your life, which is what you decided you needed, more so than hiding under any bed. And you made your choice. Oh, her face was fleshy and bright! Such an astounding faintly fleecy pleasance about her! You felt both diminished and elated when your eyes almost met on those stairs that Friday afternoon, so very long ago. Safely, sweetly, forever diminished. To joy.